The Pente Force Chronicles

Guardians of the Universe

Ann Marie R. Harvie

Out of This World
PUBLISHING

The Pente Force Chronicles: Guardians of the Universe

Cover Design:
 Acharya Hargreaves - www.acharyahargreaves.com

Inside graphics by Brian D. Murphy-brian@parttimedesign.com and by Nicole Reineke.

Out of this World Publishing owned and operated by
Ann Marie R. Harvie.
https://sites.google.com/site/outofthisworldpublishing/

Follow Ann Marie R. Harvie on Twitter @EditorYE or LinkedIn and email her at outofthisworldpublishing@gmail.com

ISBN: 978-0-692-80904-4

Published in the United States

First Printing: November 2016

Acknowledgements

Thank you...

... to my husband, Brian, who served as line editor and beta reader for this book. Thank you for always supporting my dream.

...to my children, Rachel and Ryan, who indulged their mother's need for time to write the stories.

...to my parents for throwing me outside to play with my brothers and friends so that I could use my imagination and learn to write adventurous stories.

...to my friend and advisor Nicole Reineke, who helped and encouraged me throughout this process.

...to Brian Murphy for his amazing inside artwork.

...to Pat Wysocki and Sue Douglas, two amazingly strong women who were my mentors in my early life. I wished you both could have lived to see this.

This book is dedicated to Junior, Denny, Laurie and Tori. And to Randy – as Charlie you will live forever.

Table of Contents

Introduction 1

Chapter 1 - Showdown 4

Chapter 2 - Last Wish 24

Chapter 3 - Hello, Old Friend 38

Chapter 4 - Little Soldier 48

Chapter 5 - Command Decision 60

Chapter 6 - Lamia...73

Chapter 7 - A Withering Force 88

Chapter 8 - Rescue on Daria..........................100

About the Author...111

Introduction

Hundreds of years in the future, Earth united with its ally, the planet, Zatoks, to form the Federation Chain of Life, with the sole objective of stopping Wardon, a planet bent on invading and conquering every civilization in its path.

Earth took on the task of heading Federation Defense, while the Zatokians led Federation Medicine. Other planets also took on roles of importance as they joined the Chain, sharing resources and helping strengthen the Chain's defense. Furious at the united front forming against him, Wardon's bloodthirsty Emperor, Tozar, launched a secret attack on Earth -- unleashing a biological weapon that infected many of Earth's water supplies. While the insidious chemical didn't kill those who ingested it, women were unable to bear live children.

Zatokian and Earth scientists searched frantically for a cure. One group of scientists knew of a certain Queen Moreen of Zatoks, whose blood possessed extraordinary properties that gave her incredible power. They approached Queen Moreen to ask for some of her blood in the hope that it would help develop a cure. The Queen, at first, refused; but then she remembered a fabled prophesy that declared, in the time of need, five warriors would save the universe from evil. She offered the scientists five drops of her blood, on the condition that the children born from it be given to her at the proper time for special military training. When each child, born using a chemical compound derived from those five drops of royal blood, reached the age of five, they were immersed in special forces training with the Royal Zatokian Guard.

Eventually, Chain scientists found a cure to counter Tozar's deadly biological weapon. Incensed that he would not be exterminating Earth's population after all, Tozar launched another attack. Among the targets bombed were several laboratories, including the one where the children's parents worked. The scientists died in the explosions, leaving custody of the children to Queen Moreen.

Recognizing the potential power of the children, and the need for more advanced training, Queen Moreen presented them to Richard Sanderson, head of Federation Defense. With Royal Zatokian blood running through their veins, the five genetically engineered children enjoyed enhanced speed and strength, rapid healing, and other abilities that developed as they grew older. They joined two other Special Forces teams, the Crimson Five, and the Hunters, in the fight to save the Universe from Wardon. Very quickly, the children developed into the Federation Defense's most potent and deadly special forces team, and were given the name, "The Pente Force." Along with Charlie Baker, head of the elite Federation Knights – which often provided key combat support to the special forces teams – they took on Lord Tozar in battle after battle in their fight to keep other planets free.

The Pente Force fought in many battles across many planets, and met many different species – befriending some and making enemies of others. The following stories relate some of the Pente Force's adventures...

Chapter 1 - Showdown

Star jerked her head sharply to the left. The move allowed her to dodge a deadly blue streak that came dangerously close to her head. The Special Forces commander could feel her heart pounding, almost to the rhythm of her panting as she raced through an underground Wardon Base dodging laser blasts coming at her from all directions. The adrenalinerush that fueled Star's Olympic run through enemy fire originated from an urgent need to rescue her team, the Pente Force. Their enemy, Emperor Tozar, held them captive in the base.

On the poorly lit, dank-smelling fourth level, Star ducked behind a large storage container and fired her hand-held Ks-99 laser blindly at the enemy. She needed time to think, to come up with a plan that didn't include the three platoons of Federation Knights from whom she found herself cut off.

The plan had seemed straight-forward – they would sneak into the base and then half of the troops would create a diversion while Star and the other half rescued her team. She remembered with frustration the enemy engagement that separated her from the Federation Knights and their Commander, her long-time friend Charlie Baker. The Wardons knew they were coming. Star punched the container she hid behind in frustration. It was a trap. What was she thinking? The only reason why the

Pente Force still lived is that Tozar wanted to kill them all at the same time. Of course, Tozar would know she would come! He knew if he waited long enough, she would fall into his trap and he would have them all. In some ways, her long-time enemy knew her almost as well as she knew herself.

Star flinched as a blue streak of deadly energy hit the wall behind her. The dozen Wardon soldiers who had her pinned behind the barrel were getting too close for her to stay there any longer. Grunting with the exertion, she leapt over the barrel and ran around the corner of the corridor. Laser blasts followed her, taking chunks out of the wall. Her eyes darted wildly for a place to take cover. Spotting an open door down the hall, Star opened a compartment on her holster and took out a small yellow orb the size of a golf ball. She turned the smooth orb over in her hand until she found a tiny button and pressed it. Two chemicals that were originally in separate chambers of the orb quickly began swirling together, turning the harmless orb into a deadly grenade of chemical explosives. As the orb turned a brilliant blue and Star quickly threw it around the corner. She bolted down the hall and into the room. Once inside, she slammed the door, crouched down in the far corner and covered her head. The explosion ripped through corridors, killing the soldiers, and blowing the door to the room off its hinges.

After a few minutes, Star got up and brushed the dust off her uniform. She coughed from the thick, foul-smelling smoke caused by the blast. Her entire body screamed of strained muscles and bruises, her face smudged with dirt and sweat from the exertion of dodging the Wardon soldiers. Star peeked out and saw Wardon bodies littering the floor. The orb had done its job. She could use the smoke as a cover to get to her next destination. She took just a moment to catch her breath before continuing her search.

***

One level up, Tozar felt a small tremor from the explosion and smiled, his pointed white teeth gleaming like small beacons in the dimly lit prison. The room contained four small cells; each sealed by force fields, and six larger rooms that held torture devices. Two young men, Osto and Nine, and two young women, Neptune and Pia, occupied the small cells. Tozar's eyes turned toward his captives. Their reactions to the noise of the blast betrayed what Tozar already knew – Star had arrived.

Lord Tozar waited with crazed anticipation. The short, bald ruler of Wardon had dreamed of this moment since the day he and the Pente Force first engaged in combat. He snickered. "Ah, she is coming," he said in his deep, thickly accented Wardonese voice. Most world rulers would leave such trivial matters to their generals, but not Lord Tozar. He took the Pente Force's constant interferences with his plans for universal domination personally. He would not rest until he had eliminated this enemy himself.

Tozar walked back and forth in front of the cells to examine his prizes. The greatest Special Forces team in the Universe, caught with their guard down, had been reduced to his playthings. The emperor of Wardon had indeed played with them. Bloodied and bruised from hours of torture, the team appeared tired and withdrawn from the experience.

The Wardon ruler sneered at his captives. "It's time to go," he hissed.

Tozar turned to the entrance of the prison and yelled for eight burly Dyanzian slaves. The slaves slowly shuffled mindlessly into the prison with expressionless faces and blank eyes. The eight-foot tall slaves had mind-control devices permanently implanted in their heads to ensure their complete obedience. Dyanzians had incredible strength but had been known for their kindness and passive nature. After Wardon Empire invaded their planet, all Dyanzians had mind control devices inserted into their brains. Tozar made sure any trace of humanity was erased by the devices.

"Bring them to Level 1," he ordered to his slaves. The slaves nodded numbly and walked toward the cells, carrying four sets of shackles. The team watched with weary eyes as two Dyanzians entered each cell to subdue them and take them to Level 1. It didn't take the Dyanzians long to complete their task as the team was too weak to put up much of a fight.

***

Star whispered as loudly as she dared so that the communicator in her ear would pick up her voice. "Charlie, where are you?" she demanded.

After a few moments, she heard Charlie's voice. "Where have you been!" he shouted. "I've been trying to find you for over an hour!"

"I'm trying to stay alive, thank you. The team isn't on this level either. They must be on one of the top two."

As Star spoke she could hear explosions in her earpiece. Charlie was under attack. This was all her fault. Why wouldn't he just go?

"Star, I know you don't want to hear this, but. . ."

"You're right, I don't want to hear it," she snapped, anticipating where the conversation was going.

"Look, let's get real for a second, okay? If Tozar had the chance to kill even one of you, he'd do it in a heartbeat."

"If you're so sure he's killed them already, then why did you follow me down here?" she demanded. Her eyes darted around her surroundings as she spoke in search of more enemy soldiers.

"I came to save you from yourself. I knew you'd come here no matter what Federation Defense said, so I figured I'd give you a little cover."

"Well, a lot of good you are to me down there!" she said in a frustrated voice.

Star felt she had stayed in the room too long

and feared Wardon soldiers were surrounding the door, waiting for her to poke her heard out so they could take it off.

"Star, we're stuck on the fourth level and I can't get to you. Work your way back down here. Star, please, let's pull out. We're not going to get out of here alive if we wait much longer."

"I'm not ready to give up," said Star. "You need to leave but I can't go. I know they're here - I can feel it. I know Tozar. He wants us all. I'm not leaving my team here. I'd rather die here than leaving them."

She ended the transmission abruptly to prevent any more arguments. She knew Charlie was risking his life and the lives of his Knights for her, but Star couldn't pull out. As she started to leave, she paused and took out another orb from her belt and stuck it in her boot just in case.

The dust had finally begun to settle from the earlier explosion. The orb had done its work well; part of the wall on the left side of the corridor and the catwalks above were completely blown away. Star crept back to the end of the hallway and peeked around the corner. Some of the soldiers were still alive, but they were too busy trying to dig out their comrades to notice her. She gripped her Ks-99 firmly in her left hand, turned around, and quietly crept away up to the next level of the base.

***

On the fourth level, Charlie cursed a dozen

times after Star cut off their transmission. If they made it out alive, he vowed that he was going to kill her. He was angry at her stubbornness and frustrated that she wouldn't leave with him. He was torn between finding his friends - especially his best friend Nine - and risking the lives of those he commanded for an errand that could very likely be moot. Star was his friend and he loved her. He didn't want her life to end like the others.

Charlie's rescue team had suffered moderate casualties, but had held their own against the Wardons. Because the enemy had apparently known they were coming, the Federation Knights could not advance beyond the fourth level in order to help Star. Although he tried to keep his mind on the task at hand, Charlie got knots in his stomach thinking about what could happen to his friend if Tozar got his hands on her.

***

Star started up the stairwell to the second level and ran into a Wardon soldier. She aimed quickly and shot him before he could fire his laser or alert more soldiers. It occurred to her that she would get much further if she wasn't so conspicuously dressed. She took his weapon, pulled off the enemy's clothing, donned the oversized seaweed green uniform and pulled the cap down to cover part of her face.

She exited the stairwell to the second level of the base and found the enemy running in all directions. Star heard one of them say in Wardonese that the intruders were still on the fourth level and that all available soldiers were being sent to exterminate them.

She sent a text message to Charlie to alert him that enemy reinforcements were on the way and urged him to leave the base. After sending the message, she marched down another hall, away from the chaos. She searched for a computer to give her a directory of the base. After hunting for what seemed like forever, she found one. She quickly accessed the elementary data program and pulled up the base directory. The prison was on her level in the north wing. The last log entry indicated that there were four prisoners occupying the cells. "Bingo," she said to herself as she gathered her directional bearings and headed for the prison.

***

On the fourth level, Charlie received Star's text message and pressed the button of his communicator inserted into his ear. Looking up, he saw the Wardon reinforcements starting to arrive from the other levels. He tried one last time to get her to abandon the mission. "Star, things are getting bad down here. We're going to have to pull out soon. Can you get down here?" he asked as he blasted away at the enemies pouring down the stairwells.

"I found the prison," she answered excitedly. "I'm on my way there now. Don't worry about me -- pull out now!"

"Star, I'm not leaving you. That prison is bound to be heavily guarded; you're going to need help."

"You can't help me, you're too far away. If you leave, they may think the entire rescue team is retreating and they won't search for me."

"Even if you find them, how are you going to get them out?"

Annoyance tinged Star's voice. "Will you stop trying to be a hero and please go! Don't worry about me. I'll activate the homing device on my communicator and you can pick us up on the planet's surface. Now go! You're not helping me. You've got me so worried about you I can't concentrate! Charlie, please do this for me."

Before he could protest further, Star ended the transmission. She was right -- if they didn't leave now, they would never make it. He banged his hand against the wall in frustration; he didn't want to leave her. If he did, he feared that he may not see her alive again. Charlie cursed as he signaled the remaining troops to pull back. More Wardons were coming down from the upper levels and it wouldn't be long before they were completely cut off from any escape routes. Charlie Baker and the rescue team reluctantly headed for the lower level, leaving Star alone to finish what he believed to be an impossible mission.

***

When Star arrived at the prison, she counted

six armed Wardon soldiers standing watch outside. Her stolen uniform got her five yards from the prison entrance before the soldiers drew their weapons. Once again Star opened the compartment on her belt and took out a small orb. She pressed the button and tossed it toward the guards. The bomb exploded before the soldiers had time to react.

Following the explosion, Star rushed headlong through the smoke, into the prison, and into disappointment. The prison was empty.

Star swore and punched a wall in frustration. She grew weary of the cruel game Tozar was playing. "Welcome, Commander," a thick bass voice suddenly boomed from out of nowhere. Realizing that the voice was coming from an overhead speaker, hatred welled up inside Star with such quickness and intensity it sickened her. "Where are they, Tozar?" she asked as calmly as she could.

Tozar's taunting laugh filled the prison. "Come up to the first level and join us, Commander. The set isn't complete without you."

With fatigue starting to set in, Star just wanted to confront the enemy. "I'm coming for you, Tozar," she hissed through gritted teeth. She strode out of the prison with a renewed determination to bring her friends home alive.

The first level corridors were wider and taller than the labyrinth of narrow corridors on the lower levels. The walls were also smooth and white, unlike the rough, clay walls of the lower levels. Star emerged from the stairwell, walked a little ways and stopped at the first a door. Star scanned her surroundings for another entrance, but it was the only one she could see from where she stood. Looks like only one way in, she thought. "This is not good," she sighed.

She took a deep breath and with her gun in her hand, she opened the door and stepped inside. The large auditorium's ceiling stretched to the surface of the planet. The empty room had no visible places to take cover. Star saw a large elevator of clear material on the far right wall that seemed to lead up to the surface. Tozar's escape route, she thought. She began walking towards the center of the room.

Across the room to her far left, Star suddenly noticed a large cell sealed with a force field. She fought the urge to run to it. Tozar had not yet made his appearance and the cell could be rigged with explosives. As she continued to scan the room, she discovered a catwalk halfway up the wall at the far side of the room. She saw a door in the middle of the catwalk. Next to the door stood an open, single stand elevator that extended down the ground level and upward out of sight. Star guessed Tozar would be making his entrance through there. After surveying the entire room, she concluded the larger elevator was their only way out.

Star heard the locking device on the door behind her click into place. It could only mean Tozar would come soon. She took off the uncomfortable Wardon uniform. After, she turned in the direction of her teammates to look them over, careful not to rush events by getting too close to the cell.

She winced at the sight of them; each face was bruised and swollen and their uniforms were torn and splattered with dried blood. Tears involuntarily rolled down her face when she thought of the suffering Tozar had put them through. She swore to herself that Tozar would pay for their pain.

As she predicted, Tozar made his appearance at the small elevator. His bald head gleamed with the reflection of light as he stared down at her. "I've been waiting a long time for this," he growled gleefully. "Now throw away your weapon."

Star silently obeyed and flung the weapon towards the wall.

"Your belt too," he ordered.

After Star's utility belt joined her Ks-99 laser, the emperor took the elevator down to the ground floor. He stepped off with a laser of his own in hand. His V-shaped eyebrows knitted tightly together as his face contorted into an expression of perverse satisfaction.

"This time, there is no escape," he said with maniacal joy. "My Dyanzian slaves will tear you apart while I watch. Then I'm going to blow up the base and make it your grave."

Star stared patiently at her enemy, wanting to go for his throat; but she made no move. She needed a plan, but one did not materialize. Tozar took a few tentative steps toward her. He held a remote control in his left hand and pressed the button to release the force field that held the Pente Force. With his right hand, he pointed his laser at Star. "The others are weak and will not get away from my slaves. You, however, have not been badly injured and run the risk of escape."

Tozar aimed at Star and fired his weapon. Her reflexes saved her from a mortal wound, but her dodge didn't keep her totally from harm. The blue energy blast hit her above the left hip and caused an explosion of pain. She fell to her knees with a scream and gripped her bloody side.

Tozar chuckled, and then opened the main door with the remote control. "Let the games begin," he laughed and returned to the small elevator.

Star's teammate, Nine, approached and gave his commander a hand getting up, too weak from the tortures he endured to lift her. Star groaned with the effort. She turned when she heard a door slide open next to the clear elevator. She quickly forgot about the pain when she saw the crowd of Dyanzian slaves shuffle their way towards them. Nine appeared defeated before the battle had begun. "We're not going to make it this time," he told his commander.

Star glared at him and pushed his hand off her arm, trying to ignore the searing pain that shot through her body. "I didn't come all this way to let you die."

She turned her attention to the slaves. The big, burly men moved slowly, but advanced nonetheless. They groaned incoherently as they approached the team with glazed, vacant eyes. Star counted about 25 of them -- far too many for the Pente Force to defeat in their condition, especially without weapons. Star's eyes went to her laser, but the approaching mob blocked her sight of it. She remembered the orb in her boot and an escape plan instantly materialized in her mind.

"Get back in the cell," she whispered hoarsely to her team.

The Pente Force gathered around their commander. Her order left them bewildered. "Are you nuts? We can't fight in that room. We'll be trapped," Nine protested.

Hiding in a corner while the enemy approached was not his idea of a brilliant strategy; it sounded more like suicide. The slaves blocked off their only escape route.

Star turned to face the slaves as the team moved hesitantly back to the cell. "Trust me," she said over her shoulder. "You have to do exactly as I say. Get behind the walls and cover your heads. When I tell you to, run as fast as you can to the elevator on the other side of the room, understand?"

Emerging from the catwalk, Tozar watched the Pente Force reenter the cell with a sour expression. He voiced his displeasure to Star. "I wanted more sport than this, Commander! After all these years I expected a more compelling end to your lives. You've disappointed me, cowering in a cell!"

Star walked toward the slaves. Blood saturated the lower left side of her uniform. The burning pain in her side made each step laborious. She glanced up at Tozar and allowed a smirk to creep onto her face. If it was sport he wanted, she would be more than happy to oblige him.

Star dropped to her knees. She heard her teammates shouting to her and Tozar cackling with delight. She tried to stand up twice, but fell back to her knees. She could hear the incomprehensible groans of the slaves getting closer. As she rose for the third time, she slipped her hand quickly into her boot, pulled out the orb took and pressed the button. She turned back toward the cell as fast as she could and tossed the orb at the advancing slaves.

She felt the force of the explosion on her back just as she was diving into the cell, landing on top of Pia and Osto. The sheer violence propelled Dyanzian body parts into the cell. Star's blood seemed to be saturating her uniform faster than before. Nevertheless, she got up to rally her team knowing there was no time to waste. "Now! Get to the elevator, now!" she ordered.

The Pente Force scrambled out of the cell. They nearly tripped over all the bodies that littered the room. The bomb didn't get all of them, but the few remaining slaves were slow getting up.

The team ran into the elevator. Star followed closely behind. As she approached the elevator to get in, she caught sight of Tozar out of the corner of her eye. He appeared to be struggling to get to his feet after being thrown off the catwalk from the blast. Tozar did not have his weapon. The Wardon Emperor threw a hateful glare at Star as he tried to get the elevator to come back down with a remote. He held up a self-destruct detonator and pressed the button. Alarms sounded throughout the base. A computer voice warned in Wardonese that the base would self-destruct in 30 minutes.

Star saw her opportunity to rid the universe of

Tozar forever. This was going to be it, the showdown between enemies. If she wanted to stop him once and for all, Star couldn't get on the elevator with her team. She knew it meant never seeing them again. If Tozar died with her in the base, the Wardon Empire would be crippled.

"Come on, Star, get on," said Neptune anxiously.

The Commander nodded, then turned on her communicator and signaled Charlie. "This is Star - mission complete. Fix onto my signal and come get us," she said.

Star leaned into the elevator and pressed the upper-level control, and then she took a deep breath and smashed the panel with her fist. "What are you doing? You wrecked the controls!" demanded Nine.

Star shoved her communicator into his hand. Tears filled her eyes. "You can't come with me this time," she said as she backed away from the elevator. "You'll be okay. I love you guys!"

The doors closed. Star's teammates pounded desperately on the doors in vain as the elevator made its ascent to the surface and safety. She took a painful, deep breath as she watched her friends move further away from her. When she was sure they were safe, she turned her attention to the enemy.

With her primary mission complete, Star felt free to do whatever it took to make sure Tozar didn't leave the base alive. Tozar's panicked attempts to retrieve his elevator increased as she approached. He frantically pushed the button on the remote, his head snapping between Star and the approaching elevator. Star's pain worsened and she felt a little dizzy from the loss of blood; but she continued to limp as fast as she could to get to Tozar before he could escape.

The elevator arrived and Tozar boarded. Star managed to grab a steel bar on the bottom of the ascending elevator, but she didn't have the strength to pull herself up onto the platform.

As the elevator rose to the top to Tozar's escape, he seemed oblivious to the fact that Star hung from the elevator. He screamed with surprise when her hand came up from underneath and pulled at his leg. He tried to pry her fingers from him, but he couldn't loosen her death grip.

"I win, Tozar," she said as she yanked him off the elevator. His high-pitched scream echoed in her ear as he fell past her. It took all of her remaining strength, but Star pulled herself onto the elevator as it reached the top. Tozar's flailing arms and legs were the last thing she remembered.

***

When the Pente Force arrived at the surface, Charlie and some of his soldiers met them with a waiting shuttle. Star's absence devastated Charlie. He had to fight the urge to travel down the elevator shaft and try to rescue her. The Pente Force begged to go back down to the base and save their commander before it self-destructed, but Charlie and his soldiers quickly whisked them into the shuttle.

Charlie put a hand on his best friend's shoulder as the shuttle lifted off. "There's nothing we can do," he said with a choked voice. "It's going to blow. I'm sorry."

Charlie remembered Star telling him not to be a hero. He wished she had practiced what she preached. Just as the shuttle left the surface, the planet shook violently. A large cloud of smoke appeared at the location of the base, shooting debris up in the air.

***

Hours after the smoke from the explosion settled, only a gaping crater remained of the Wardon base. They found Star close to the hole. Her body, bloody and bruised, was sprawled out on the grass as if she were a doll discarded by a child. It wasn't until Charlie picked her up and heard a slight, raspy breath that they discovered she was still alive.

They rushed Star to the shuttle and headed for a nearby Federation station. Medical technicians treated her for critical internal wounds and broken bones. Doctors were unable to determine if she would live or die for weeks. When her condition finally stabilized, her friends and teammates breathed a long sigh of relief.

***

Weeks later, Star explained her last real memory was of Tozar falling, but she vaguely recalled crawling out of a small opening just before the base blew up. Charlie told her Tozar's body had not been recovered. Star frowned. "That's impossible. I saw him fall. I barely got out and I had used the elevator," she said.

"His body didn't turn up, Star. I'm not saying he made it out, I'm just telling you Federation Defense couldn't find his body in the rubble. It could've been thrown into the forest; in which case, we might never find it," said Charlie.

Star frowned. She knew better; the little space slug somehow got away from her once again. Perhaps the fall wasn't as far down as her delirious mind thought. He could have made it out of the room and somehow took cover or got out another way. Despite her apparent failure to rid the universe of Tozar once and for all, all was not lost. Charlie and the team were all right, and she was relatively in one piece. She could try again another time. Next time, she hoped, it would be the final time.

Chapter 2 - Last Wish

Parachute silk rustled in the night wind. Neptune concentrated for any sound beyond the soft flapping of the material as she quickly stuffed the parachute back into its bag. Palladin struggled to do the same. They'd dropped about a hundred yards beyond the perimeter of the Wardon base. With the parachute back in its bag, she turned to Palladin — and froze. His shirt had pulled up as he wrenched off his jump harness. In the light of Saffron's moon, she could see a glint of metal across his chest.

"What are you some kind of android?"

Neptune eyed the body plate that covered Palladin's chest. He struggled to pull his shirt down. It was too late. She saw the plate, even in the darkness.

"No, I'm not an android," he said as he turned away. "It's a body plate to protect my synthetic lungs. They had to remove part of my rib cage to fit them in."

Neptune fought back her annoyance. Why was she being punished? Why did Federation Defense stick her with someone clearly not in peak condition for this mission? The fleet was standing off the Saffron system, waiting for Palladin to disable the field generator that protected the Wardon base. Based on what she had just seen, she had serious doubts that he was up to the task. "Oh, that's just great," she said in an angry whisper. "You're probably going to drop dead on me. I don't understand why I had to take you with me."

Neptune threw her chute pack to the ground in a rage and ran a hand through her short, brown hair. Palladin stepped up to her, his face inches from hers. His green eyes flashed with anger. Neptune held her ground. "I didn't come with you. You came with me, Captain. This is my mission. You're supposed to cover me while I disable the field generator. Remember that!"

Neptune's brown eyes narrowed. "Then lead the way, Sport. I'll cover you."

Her tone made Palladin step back. He stared at her for moment and the anger washed away from his face. Finally, he moved past her and jogged towards the enemy base. Neptune pulled out her Ks-99 and followed her charge.

They were only minutes from their destination. They hid behind a bush a couple of feet from the base. The soft warm wind ruffled the leaves on the trees. They were alone — not one patrol in the area. To Neptune that meant two things -- the Wardons were overly confident about the invincibility of their base and they hadn't detected the Federation Defense fleet that would reach the Saffron System in an hour to blow the base right off the planet.

Palladin pulled out a hand scanner. Almost immediately lights began to dance across the device's monitor. Palladin watched the readings carefully. A Federation spy satellite had detected a slight fluctuation in the force field protecting the base every six minutes. The fluctuation lasted only seconds. Neptune and Palladin would have to slip through the force field to get into the base to disable the field generator.

As Neptune waited, she visually scanned the area again for foot soldiers, but found none. Her eyes went to the massive black stronghold in front of her and the grate on the ventilation duct they were supposed to crawl through to get to the generator. Neptune felt a wave of anxiety as she stared at the biggest base she had ever seen. Partially underground to disguise its enormous size, the enemy fortress was the size of a small city. The exposed portion of the base had a smooth looking texture and a dome shape. The force field protecting the base made a soft, pulsing sound that was almost hypnotic. Palladin's voice broke her concentration. "So why did you join Special Forces?"

Neptune hesitated. It was a painful story and she didn't like to tell it. "Let's just say I was born to be part of the Pente Force."

Palladin didn't look up from the scanner. Neptune could see his face in the glow of the machine. He appeared to be in his early twenties, about the same age as Neptune. His sickness paled his skin, but it didn't affect his good looks. However, his grating personality rendered his light brown hair and green eyes a little less handsome to her.

Palladin's tragedy was known throughout Federation Defense. He had contracted a mysterious disease during an attack on a Wardon Laboratory. His vital organs were rotting away and the

Federation doctors were replacing them with synthetic ones. Still, it was only a matter of time before other precious organs that could not be duplicated with synthetics would be affected. "I didn't really have a choice either at first. You know, with my dad being the great General Keefer and all," said Palladin.

Neptune's tone turned resentful. "You should've gotten out when you got sick. Now you're risking my life, not to mention the fleet, by being here. What if you have some sort of weird attack? I'm no doctor. What am I supposed to do with you?"

Palladin looked up from his scanner. His eyes locked on to hers, his sincerity genuine. Something clicked inside Neptune. She couldn't put her finger on it. The feeling made her nervous, but she didn't look away. "That won't happen, I promise you. But I'll tell you a little secret — my kidneys are beginning to fail, and I have to have them replaced. This will be my last mission."

The scanner went dark and Palladin's head snapped back to the machine. "Now. Go now!" he said. Neptune shot up and ran for the ventilation duct with Palladin right behind her.

They crawled through the duct for a few feet before they stopped. A warm, constant breeze passed through the duct and made the air comfortable. There was adequate room for crawling in the duct, but not a lot for maneuvering around. Neptune looked back to watch Palladin punch a new command into his scanner. The new setting would lead them to the generator by picking up its energy readings. When he finished he nodded to Neptune as a signal to continue. The pair proceeded cautiously. Every few feet they came upon grated panels where the air would blow into the many rooms of the base. As Neptune looked down at the enemy when she passed each grate, her hate mounted. Visions of Wardons killing her family and friends flashed in her mind, fueling already intense emotions. So many people died because of them. She wanted to jump through the grate and attack, but she fought the urge and continued. When the time was right, she would make them all pay.

Palladin's scanner continued to lead them closer to the generator. Neptune tried to review the mission in her head, but Palladin kept interrupting her thoughts with his whispering. "So, this is what the Special Forces do, huh? Are you always sent in before the fleet?"

"Shh! Stop jabbering! Yes, this is what we do. You know that!"

"We may not get the chance to talk later. I just want to get to know you better."

Neptune's aggravation mounted. This wasn't a date – their lives and the lives of millions depended on this mission. Why was he doing this? She stopped and turned to him, her face red with anger. "Palladin, be quiet! We're going to get caught!"

In the dim light illuminating from the grates, she could see sadness in his green eyes. She let out a defeated sigh and shook her head. "Why did I get picked for this assignment anyway?"

She continued to crawl through the duct, not

expecting an answer.

"I picked you."

Neptune's anger turned to surprise. She stopped with a start and looked back to Palladin. He picked her? How could he have picked her? Her assignments came directly from the head of Federation Defense. Then Neptune felt something -- it felt like closeness, something she only shared with a select few. But why him? Why now? Before she could say anything, the scanner flashed.

"This is it," said Palladin as he moved past her to the grate just ahead.

Neptune shook off all the questions in her head and approached the grate. She peered down and saw three Wardon technicians working on the massive generator on the far right of the room. "Here we go," said Palladin in a whisper.

Neptune nodded and signaled for him to be quiet. She pulled up the grate as quietly as she could to get a better look. She poked her head out of the opening in the duct. They were about 10 feet up from the floor and about 15 feet from the technicians. The generator was making the pulsating sound she had heard outside, but now it was much louder. She decided she would use that to her advantage. She looked around the large room and found no one else inside. The door was closed. *Easy stuff* she thought.

Neptune jumped out of the duct and landed on the ground in a squat position, followed by Palladin. The technicians were so engrossed in their work, they didn't see them. Neptune straightened and walked towards them. Palladin stayed behind and let her do her job.

She stood five feet from the technicians and cleared her throat loudly enough to be heard through the hum of the generator. She couldn't shoot them in the back. She wanted the enemy to see the satisfaction on her face when she killed them. All three turned around. Three quick blasts shot from the Ks-99 aimed directly for their hearts hit their mark. Blood quickly saturated the enemies' uniforms and their gray skin began to pale from the blood loss. The anguished expression on the enemies' faces quieted the rage Neptune felt since she had entered the base. The technicians fell dead before they could reach for weapons or a communicator.

As Palladin approached, Neptune pulled one of the dead technicians off the generator controls where he'd fallen. She did so without emotion; all her hate temporarily vanished. Palladin wore an expression of admiration for her quick, neat performance, but Neptune pretended to ignore it. She struggled to dislike him, but couldn't. It made her uncomfortable. There was something about him. When he wasn't being a jerk, he was almost charming. "It's all yours," she said casually as she walked to the door.

The humming sound from the generator had muffled the blasts from her weapon, but she put her ear to the door to make sure she hadn't attracted attention. When she heard nothing out of the ordinary, she breathed a sigh of relief and locked the door.

As she walked back to the generator, Neptune could see Palladin holding on to his lower back as he used the other to work. The jump from the vent must have aggravated his condition. A feeling of sadness washed over her. He was rotting away slowly. His father would replace the organs with synthetic ones until he turned Palladin into an android. She didn't want that to happen to him. She realized that despite her best efforts he'd become her partner and she cared about him.

"Are you in a lot of pain?" she asked.

Palladin continued with his work but took his hand off his back. "I'll be fine," he said, trying unsuccessfully to mask his pain as he worked.

Neptune's eyebrows knitted in curiosity. "Why are you here, Palladin? I mean, why did you take this mission?"

Palladin stepped up to another part of the generator, never taking his eyes off his work. "I always wanted my dad to be proud of me, but I messed up in the battle on Fantastica when I caught this disease. I wanted a Special Forces assignment to redeem myself. I made my father promise me this last assignment before I left the service. Call it a soldier's last wish."

"You wanted to be a hero?"

Palladin let out a slight laugh. "To you, this is just another job. But this was my last chance to make my dad proud."

"Why did you pick me?"

Palladin stopped his work and looked into her eyes for a moment. Then his gaze went to the three bodies. "Because I think you're amazing."

Neptune stared at him in disbelief as his gaze turned from the bodies back to her. He blushed and looked away. It said everything. Neptune realized why the connection was so strong — the feeling came from both of them. She felt a red flush come over her cheeks, too, and was glad he had turned away. Palladin continued with his work as he made his confession. "I saw you with your team in the hangar bay at Beta Control when I first started my training. Ever since then I've followed your career. I know every battle you've fought, every medal you've won."

Neptune's heart sank a little as she recalled the cost of some of those battles. She turned to go back to the door. The loss of friends in those battles made the victories empty.

"Have you also kept track of every friend that I've lost in those battles?" she asked bitterly.

Palladin kept adjusting the generator. He took a tool from the belt of one of the dead technicians. "I've admired your skill and your courage, Neptune. But what I don't admire is your attitude. You hate too much. I know your story as well as you know mine. I know they've hurt you, but you don't let anyone help you deal with it. You push people away; I've seen you do it to your own teammates. You've got to control the hate before it eats you alive like this disease is eating me."

Neptune turned from the door and stared

angrily at him. She wanted to yell at him and tell him to mind his own business, but she couldn't. He was right. But she couldn't control the rage within her. No use arguing about it. She said nothing and turned back to the door.

Time was running out. The fleet would be coming into the Saffron air space soon, and they had to meet the stealth retriever in 20 minutes. She was tempted to just throw an orb bomb in the generator, but that would risk only a partial shutdown. There would be no chance to return and finish the job. Palladin, she was told, had a special talent with Wardon generators and would ensure a complete and permanent job.

Just as Neptune opened her mouth to yell for Palladin to hurry up, the humming sound stopped. Time to go. She ran beneath the duct opening and pulled a table over to help Palladin climb up. He just made it through the duct when the door crashed open. Five Wardon soldiers entered with their weapons drawn. They spotted Neptune and began to fire. She couldn't jump up on the table to escape. She ran to the generator for cover, firing at the enemy as she went, killing one of the soldiers.

Suddenly, Palladin jumped out of the duct and began firing on the enemy and killed two more. Neptune felt a cold shiver go through her as she watched her unlikely hero try to save her.

"Palladin, no!"

Neptune's cry came too late. Palladin allowed himself to become wide open and an easy target. One of the Wardon soldiers took aim and fired at him while the other continued to fire on Neptune.

Palladin had the opportunity to dodge the blast, but didn't. Neptune watched the whole thing as if in slow motion. Palladin saw the soldier take aim and it seemed as if he lowered his weapon slightly and held his head up high and waited.

The laser caught him in the chest plate. Palladin fell on his back onto the table. Neptune's body went numb for a split second as she watched him fall. She turned to her enemy with a renewed hate. In her rage, she wanted to take on the whole base and just keep shooting until they cut her down. Then she thought of the possibility that Palladin might still be alive. If he was, he would need her help.

More soldiers would come soon. Neptune took an orb bomb out of a compartment on her belt and turned the yellow ball over in her hand. She found the button she was looking for and pressed it, releasing a second chemical into the yellow liquid. The orb turned a brilliant blue. She threw it at the soldiers and ducked behind the disabled generator and waited.

The bomb resulted in a loud explosion and heavy smoke. The blast killed the soldiers and caused part of the ceiling to cave in. The rubble blocked the entrance and bought Neptune a little time before other soldiers could come in to investigate.

Neptune ran for Palladin. He was still alive and conscious, but she could see that the chest plate was badly damaged. Neither said anything. With all the strength they had left, both managed to get into the duct and shut the grate. Neptune had to drag Palladin through the duct and out of the base to the stealth retriever. No guards pursued them. Neptune's plan had worked.

Neptune held Palladin's hand as the stealth retriever set course to rendezvous with the fleet. Thanks to him, the fleet could destroy the base from space. The Wardon Empire would have no time to send out its warships to defend it.

Palladin shook in pain, but he squeezed Neptune's hand and smiled. She couldn't smile back. Tears welled in her eyes. As hard as she fought it, she had grown very fond of him in a short period of time. Now he was dying. Like her other friends, he would only be a memory and a headstone on Warrior's Hill. Moments like this happened too often in her life. "You knew you were never coming back."

"If I went back, my father would've turned me into a machine. I wanted to die like a man."

A couple of tears fell from Neptune's face onto his hand as she shook her head. "You're going to die a hero."

Palladin gave her another weak smile. "That was my true last wish. I'm so glad you were by my side when it happened."

Neptune wiped away her tears, only to have more appear. "Why did you do this to me? Why did you get me to care if you knew you were going to die on me?"

Palladin's face had no color and sweat poured down his face. He didn't have much time. "I've wanted to meet you since I first saw you. But you hated me and you didn't even know me. That's when I knew we could help each other. Just for a while, I got to be close to you, and you stopped hating long enough to care about someone."

Palladin's body convulsed and sparks from his short circuiting synthetic lungs shot out of his body. He tried to suppress a scream of pain. He squeezed Neptune's hand and she began to cry. As he faded away, he whispered, "They are the enemy, but your hate for them is consuming you. Don't hate them so much."

Palladin closed his eyes and died.

Neptune touched his forehead with hers. Her new friend was gone. Anyone she ever cared for was taken by the Wardon Empire. His mission for her had failed -- he asked the impossible. As her tears fell on his face, she whispered, "You've just given me a reason to hate them more."

Chapter 3 - Hello, Old Friend

Star bolted down the dimly lit corridors of the space cruiser, <u>Black Widow</u>. Her heart pounded in her ears as she ran, blocking out the soft, pulsating sounds of the ship's engines. The fear of being too late kept her marathon run through the winding halls at a lightning clip as she rushed to the man she was supposed to protect from a deadly assassin.

She had left Ezra of Reah for only a short time to do a thorough security check of the area. When she'd tried to contact the four guards posted outside his chambers, she'd received no answer -- the enemy had struck.

Star saw the blood-soaked bodies of the guards lying near the door to Ezra's chamber. She slowed her pace to a cautious walk. Pulling out her Ks-99 laser, she pressed herself against the cold corridor wall. The freezing metal penetrated her beige federation uniform and sent a chill through her body. She cursed herself a dozen times for leaving the planet leader. Ezra had petitioned for membership in the Federation Chain of Life and it was her duty to protect him from the Wardon Empire on the trip to Earth.

Wardon had been making more frequent attacks on Ezra's planet and he was considering joining the Federation Chain of Life for protection. Thinking of how she'd failed him, it was difficult for Star to steady her breathing and calm herself for the inevitable confrontation.

The index finger on her left hand automatically released the safety from the Ks-99, and then settled back to its familiar place on the trigger. Star put her ear to the door of Ezra's chamber. She heard struggling noises inside the cabin and then a sudden, loud thump. Star took in a deep breath, slid the access card through the lock and leapt inside.

"Freeze!" she ordered.

Both of her hands were on her Ks-99 as she crouched down close to the wall to dodge any incoming laser fire. It was dark inside the cabin and her eyes had to adjust to the lack of light. A death-like silence filled the chamber. She caught a sudden movement in the corner of her eye and turned her head. Her eyes quickly became accustomed to the dark and she was able to see shapes inside the cabin. A shadowed figure leaned over a couch. As she watched, it yanked up another figure to a sitting position.

"Lights!" barked Star to the cabin's computer as she moved closer to the wall, certain her command would bring at least a couple of laser blasts from the intruder's weapon.

The voice-activated computer complied and the lights came on. She saw the intruder held Ezra, unconscious but alive, as a human shield on the couch.

Fire-red hair flowed in thick waves down to the young woman's shoulders. Her bright green eyes blazed with anger. She held her laser to Ezra's head, balancing him with her left arm. Blood streamed down his face and into his dark mustache and beard.

It took a moment for the intruder's face to register in Star's mind. When it did, she couldn't believe her eyes. *Tessa*. But that was impossible. She fell eight months ago during the battle against Wardon on the planet Mars. The intruder's eyes widened for just a moment and Star knew that she recognized her as well.

"Tessa?" whispered Star, almost to herself.

An unfamiliar anger flashed in Tessa's eyes and she pushed the muzzle of her blaster harder into Ezra's temple. "Move and he gets it," she declared, narrowing her eyes into tiny slits.

Star felt as if she had just been punched in the stomach. Tessa had been one of her closest friends. Why was a Federation Knight and the daughter of a highly decorated general working for Wardon? Despite her disbelief, Star remained in her attack stance, her weapon aimed directly between Tessa's eyes.

"Surrender," she ordered.

She struggled to keep her emotions from surfacing. Her heart raced as her confusion and disbelief began to consume her. Was this her enemy? Should she shoot the woman with whom she'd been through so much? Memories flooded her mind of battles where the two fought side-by-side. The good times when they'd defeated the enemy, and sad times when they'd buried friends at Warriors Hill on Earth. What was going on? For the first time in her military career, Star, the Federation's best, didn't know what to do.

Tessa's face revealed an internal battle of her own. She seemed to be struggling to keep her angry expression; she also seemed to be fighting back tears. "Back off, Star," said Tessa. "I came for him, not you. Leave now and I'll let you live."

Star stayed in position, her Ks-99 never wavering. "Release the leader," Star ordered. "Traitor."

Tessa blinked as if she'd been smacked out of a trance. "I'm not a traitor," she replied in a shaky voice. Her expression softened and the hate in her eyes gradually faded. "Whatever you think right now, Star, I'm not a traitor."

Star straightened from her defensive crouch, though she kept her blaster at Tessa's head. Star felt a sharp pang of anger. "Oh no? You go missing from your unit and when you surface you've got a gun to an allied Leader's head! What do you call that?"

Star could not will her heart to stop slamming against her chest. She struggled unsuccessfully to steady her breathing. Her hands, while still on her gun, were cold and clammy. She battled with herself to keep them steady. She didn't want to believe her eyes, but facts were facts. "You are a Wardon assassin and a traitor."

Tessa's voice was urgent, her expression panicked. "I'm not! I don't want to do this. I have to."

An explanation for the bizarre situation suddenly popped into Star's head. Of course! She wasn't doing this of her own free will. She was being *made* to kill for them. "You can surrender. You don't have to kill for them anymore. I can help you."

Tessa's eyes watered and her breathing quickened. Her gaze darted around the room as if she was in a hurry.

"I can't surrender, Star. You can't help me. I'm not the old Tessa," she said in a soft whisper. Tears began to stream down her face. "I've been changed."

Star furrowed her brows in confusion. She took a step toward her friend.

"Stay back!" Tessa ordered angrily as she nudged her blaster against the unconscious leader's head.

"What do you mean changed? I don't understand."

Tessa's face paled. Her breathing came in quick shallow breaths as she explained to Star the horror of her capture at Mars by the enemy. She'd tried to escape, but could not. Wardon's methods of torture were excruciating and Tessa was caught each time she attempted suicide.

"They tortured me, Star," she said in an agonized tone. "Oh God, it was pure hell."

Listening to Tessa's ordeal caused tears to well up in Star's eyes. Tessa continued her horrifying story, describing how the Wardon scientists had implanted an organic mind-control device in her head. She said she could feel it wrap around her brain. When the Wardons gave her orders, the device made sure she obeyed. It would inflict a pain so great Tessa would almost go insane and would have to comply.

Star could feel her face heat with anger. Wardon scum, she thought. She became more determined than ever to help her friend. "I can help, Tessa," she said. "Just put the gun down. We're not far from a Federation base. We can get that thing out of your head."

Tessa let out a frustrated breath. "You don't understand! I must finish my mission!"

Once again, anger flashed in her green eyes and Star knew the thing in her head was taking over. Star didn't know what to do. She could not release Tessa. She wanted to help her friend, but her first priority was Ezra's safety. Duty had to come first.

"I can't let you take him," said Star. "You know I can't. Let me help you, Tessa. I'm still your friend. Please trust me."

Tessa took a deep breath and let it out. Her expression changed from angry to sad. It seemed that for the moment she had won the battle for her mind. She gazed at her friend for what seemed like forever. Sweat beaded on Tessa's forehead as her breath quickened. "Star, no matter what, you can't let my father and sisters think I am a traitor," she said as she removed the blaster from Ezra's head and placed it against her own.

She let go of Ezra, letting his unconscious form fall softly onto the couch. "Tessa don't," shouted Star.

Before she could pull the trigger, Tessa's face contorted as if in horrible pain. She screamed in agony and blood poured from her nose. With one hand, she grabbed her own head while she tried to pull the laser's trigger with the other. "Leave me alone!" she screamed. "I'm not going to do it!"

Star didn't know what command the thing in Tessa's head was giving, but she couldn't stand the torture her friend's agony. Concern for Tessa overruled caution and Star lowered her weapon. She moved toward her friend to help her.

Tessa let go of her head and straightened. Blood red corneas circled her green eyes pupils. Her face contorted into a maniacal expression. The mind control had taken over. Star saw the same thing on the faces of Dyanzian Warriors turned Wardon slaves. Star's heart sank. Tessa pointed her blaster at Star, though it shook violently in her hand. She squeezed her eyes shut and let out a cry of agony. "No!" she screamed at the ceiling. "I'm not killing for you anymore!"

Tessa grabbed her right arm with her left hand as she desperately fought to control herself. She was able to jerk the gun enough to prevent a fatal shot, but it went off just the same and shot Star in the right arm. Star fell back.

Star's many years of intensive training took over. She jumped to her feet in an attack position. Her left hand rose, and shot Tessa in the chest before she had time to think about it. She instantly regretted what she did.

"Tessa!" she cried as the redhead fell to the floor behind the couch. Star stumbled to her friend's side to see a pool of blood quickly forming on the floor.

Tessa's face was quickly paling from the loss of blood. She flashed a smile at Star; death was imminent and she seemed at peace. Soon there would be no more pain. Tears streamed down Star's face. Had she not attacked, Star could have saved Tessa; she just knew it.

"Tessa! I'm so sorry. I didn't mean to!" she cried.

"It's okay. They wanted me to kill you. I could've killed the leader; I had no feelings for him. But I couldn't kill my oldest friend," Tessa wheezed.

The bloodstain on the carpet grew at a rapid rate. Star tried to apply pressure to the wound, but try as she might Star could not save her friend. "I'm not a traitor. I killed because I couldn't control myself. I love the Chain of Life and I love my father, you know that."

Tessa's body convulsed and Star cradled her friend in her arms. "I know. It's not your fault. I'll tell him. He'll understand," she said. Tessa said nothing else. Her body shook once more and became still.

***

Star delivered Ezra safely to Earth and soon after his planet became the newest addition to the Federation Chain of Life. Star also returned Tessa's body to Federation Defense and gave her report. An autopsy uncovered the mind control device, but the scientists could not find a way of destroying it to save others. There was much debate about Tessa's assassination attempt. Star testified that the situation was out of Tessa's control and with the autopsy report she cleared her friend's name. Federation Defense declared Tessa a heroine for her part in the battle of Neptune and posthumously awarded her the Gold Medal of Bravery, which Star delivered to her family. The declaration enabled Tessa to be buried at Warrior's Hill, a place of honor for Federation soldiers. Gen. Hunter's unparalleled grief shattered his and his remaining daughters' relationship with Star. She had once been considered a member of the family. Killing Tessa made her a murderer in their eyes. They did not accept Star's account of what happened.

A month after Tessa's death, Star visited her grave underneath a large oak tree that overlooked many rows of white tombstones. Star replayed her last encounter with Tessa in her mind, as she had done dozens of times. She gazed out at the other headstones that seemed to stretch on forever. "I'll join you one day, old friend," she said to the headstone with a sigh. "But not until I take half the Wardon empire with me."

Chapter 4 - Little Soldier

Standing on top of a large, dirt hill on the small moon of Cria, Star stared at the fading sunset. Smoke from the destruction of an entire civilization muddied the pinkish illumination the Crian sun tried to paint in the sky. Star could feel the rumble of the earth beneath her boots as explosions reverberated in the distance.

Finally, she took her eyes away from the horizon and gazed down at the raging battle below her. Federation Defense began losing ground to overwhelming Wardon forces only a few miles away from the Crian royal palace. They would have to pull out soon before Wardon reinforcements arrived. Anger filled her. They had lost Cria and Star hated losing.

Cria and its population were somewhat of a mystery to the Federation. The royal family had only petitioned for membership in the Federation Chain of Life a year ago and little had been discovered about Cria or its people prior to Wardon's invasion. *All those innocent lives lost*, thought Star angrily. *What a waste*.

Star felt an overwhelming urge to take her team and go down to the desert and start killing Wardons. But she knew she couldn't go. She had another mission. The Crian Emperor and his wife were off planet on a diplomatic mission when the invasion began. Their daughter did not go with them.

Mina, the five-year-old heir to the now obliterated throne had been left behind with a nurse. The Emperor begged the Federation to rescue his child. Mina was not among the Crians rescued from the palace before Wardon soldiers laid waste to it. However, rescued Crians who worked in the palace swore the girl remained alive inside. This hit a nerve with Star. As a child, Star successfully hid from the Wardons as they destroyed her parents' laboratory. She knew it was possible that Mina could still be alive. Star had received orders to recover her -- dead or alive -- before Federation Defense retreated.

Star felt a strong arm encircle her waist from behind. She turned from the battle to see Lucien, a fellow Special Forces soldier and her love, smiling down at her. She did not smile back. Not even he could ease her anxiety over the mission, although having him with her would be a big help. Lucien had been ordered to go in with her to help search for Mina. One of the few things the Federation did know about the Crians was that they had telepathic abilities. Lucien would be able to use his telepathic abilities to be able to find and communicate with the child. "It's time to go," he said softly.

Star put her head on his chest and squeezed him tight. "I don't want to find a dead kid," she said wearily.

Lucien kissed the top of her head. "Let's go. Mina's waiting."

Star nodded and took a deep breath as she followed him down the hill to the transport.

***

Federation soldiers kept the majority of the Wardon army busy in the desert near the palace. However, Wardon soldiers still occupied the damaged building. A squadron of Federation Knights would provide the diversion to allow them to get into the palace. She and Lucien waited for the signal.

Suddenly it happened - explosions shook the ground and illuminated the darkened sky. In the ensuing chaos, Star could see the Wardons inside the palace scramble out to engage their enemy.

Star and Lucien sprinted to the back of the palace to a blown out window. Star peeked through the window and watched the gray-skinned humanoids with the bushy V-shaped eyebrows rush past the window to the front of the palace. She squatted down next to Lucien and gave him a thumb's up. She cautiously climbed through the window and Lucien followed. Star gripped her Ks-99 laser firmly in her left hand and ducked into the empty study nearby. With Lucien right behind her, she quietly shut the door.

Star turned to her telepathic companion. "Are we close enough? Can you tell?" she whispered.

Lucien's sky blue eyes lost focus as he concentrated. He seemed a million miles away, but she knew he was calling to Mina. She held her breath. After what seemed like hours, he returned from his trance and smiled. "She's alive. She's upstairs in her bedroom. Poor thing's terrified."

Star let out a sigh of relief. "Okay, let's go get

her and get the hell out of here."

She opened the door and cautiously poked her head out to check her bearings. It took her a moment to remember the floor plan of the now ransacked palace she had studied earlier. Tapestries hung in shreds and remnants of chandeliers clung to the ceiling partially lighting the place. The stench of death permeated the air as did the smoke and sounds of the bombs exploding outside. Bodies of dead Crians littered the floor. Star's gaze fell to a corpse wearing a nurse's uniform.

The diversion created by the Knights kept the Wardons busy. Star turned to Lucien and signaled him to follow her. They sprinted across the large hall, jumping over bodies and debris, and headed to the stairs leading to the second floor. After ducking behind a couch to let a group of Wardons run by to join the battle outside, Star and Lucien bounded up the stairs to the bedrooms. Star ran past the first two rooms on the second floor. Out of the corner of her eye, she saw Lucien stop at the second room. She returned and he nodded, confirming Mina was inside. She pressed her ear against the door to listen for noises. She didn't hear anything. "Are you sure?" she mouthed silently to Lucien.

He nodded, and then turned to make sure no Wardons were coming up the stairs. Star turned the knob of the door and the two of them stepped inside.

Broken toys and little girl's clothes littered the floor of the large room. Laser burns scorched the pastel pink walls. Star could still smell the laser discharge. A small night-light gave a soft illumination. Star eyed an empty closet across from the bed. She frowned. The Wardons had already searched the room. Star turned to Lucien. "She's not here," she whispered.

She could hear the explosions outside and knew they didn't have much time before Federation Defense retreated. Lucien hadn't heard her. He closed his eyes for an instant and opened them. "She's under the bed," he whispered.

Star observed the queen-sized bed. The quilts and bedspread had been ripped off and discarded on the floor. Star put her weapon in her holster and knelt down for a closer look.

She saw nothing but an empty floor. She looked up at the base of the bed, but could not see anything in the darkness. "Mina, it's okay. You can come out," coaxed Star in Universal language. "Mommy and Daddy sent us to come get you."

A sudden movement made Star jump back. Before she knew it, a tiny body fell from its hiding spot and skidded out from under the bed to the other side and went into the closet. Star got up and carefully approached.

Mina reminded Star of a china doll she had long ago – tiny, and dressed in a pink nightgown and slippers. Her curly black tresses fell to her shoulders and her milky white face had a smattering of pink on each cheek.

Mina's big, violet eyes filled with fear. The closer Star got to the closet, the more frightened she became. Star watched as Mina finally slid down to the bottom of the closet and hugged her shaking body. She felt Lucien's hand on her arm. "Star, she's scared because you're not telepathic. She's talking to you, but you're not answering. Let me try," he said.

Mina's reaction left no doubt in Star's mind that she had witnessed a great deal of violence during the invasion and possibly saw the Wardons kill her nurse. Star wanted the Wardons to pay for taking the innocence away from Mina the way they took it from her. But for now, they needed to get out of the palace. She stepped back from the shaking child. "It's okay, I won't touch you."

Lucien approached the child and smiled in a way that always made Star feel at ease. She could tell that he and Mina were communicating. Soon a change seemed to come over Mina. She appeared more relaxed and came out of the closet. Star wanted to leave as soon as possible but didn't want Mina to see the carnage outside. "Wrap her up in a blanket, Lucien, so she doesn't see what's outside," she said.

He nodded and held out his hand. Mina stared pensively at Star for a moment. Then she took Lucien's hand, her little one lost in his, and he walked her over to the quilts. Star went to the window and peered down at the battle at the other end of the palace. She pressed a button on her communicator. "This is Star. We've found the girl. We're going to need a transport to get her away from the palace. Head on over with one of the tanks," she said. She didn't wait for a response before she cut the transmission.

When Star left the window, Lucien had Mina in

his arms wrapped in a blanket. "Let's get out of here," she said as she stepped over toys to open the door. She pulled out her weapon and walked out in front.

They made it halfway down the stairs when about ten Wardon soldiers spotted them. Star took in a quick breath and then started a hasty retreat. "Quick, back upstairs!" said Star as she pushed Lucien.

They bolted up the stairs with the Wardons in hot pursuit. Star turned and fired to cover Lucien. She killed one, sending him reeling into the others and knocking them down. She continued up the stairs while dodging the flurry of badly aimed blue streaks coming at her.

Star immediately closed the door to the first bedroom containing Lucien and Mina. Lucien pushed a dresser in front of the door. Star gazed down at the pint-sized princess who stared at her blankly. Star gave the child a quick, uneasy smile.

Lucien ran past Star to the window. He looked down and slammed his palms against the wall with a curse. They picked the wrong room to escape from the Wardons. "We're trapped. We can't get out through the window," he said.

Star came up next to him and saw the long drop and flaming debris. She searched but failed to find an alternative exit. She didn't count on the debris blocking their escape. Her attention turned to the banging at the bedroom door. A knot tightened in her stomach.

Star glanced at Mina who watched the door.

The child showed no emotion. Star worried that the experience had been too much for Mina and that she had gone catatonic. "What's with her?" asked Star.

"She's fine. I told her that we were her friends and that she had to be brave for us so we could get her to her parents. That's her brave face," said Lucien in a whisper. He paused for a moment. "I can't tell her she's not going to get out of here."

Star shot him an angry look. "Don't write us off yet."

She marched past Lucien, scooped Mina up and placed her on the other side of the large bed. She knelt down and talked to the child at eye level. "Now listen to me, Mina. There are bad men outside that door. You have to be brave now more than ever. Stay behind us okay? We're going to try to blast our way out."

Suddenly, the Wardons began firing through the door and the dresser. Star and Lucien dove for the wall. Lucien didn't move fast enough and caught a laser blast in his right side. The shot sent him reeling towards the other wall several feet from the bed. Star couldn't get to him from her position without getting shot. She tried to call her team on her communicator. "This is Star, we need assistance. We're trapped on the second floor east wing. Lucien's hit. Somebody get in here quick!"

Star returned the Wardon's fire, shooting blindly at the dresser, taking pieces out of it with each blast. Star turned for a moment to see Mina run to Lucien and hug him tightly. Blood began to saturate his uniform. His eyes locked onto Star's. His face contorted in pain. "Star," he called. "I can't move. Prop me up and I'll help you."

His Ks-86 laser landed across the room when he fell. Star couldn't risk retrieving the weapon. She turned away from him and focused her attention on the door. "Stay there and take care of Mina," she shouted as she continued to fire.

More laser blasts came through the door and dresser, taking chunks out of the bed and mattress where Mina had once been. Panic momentarily gripped Star. Her team might not make it to them in time and Lucien couldn't help her. How was she going to get them out?

Star fought back her emotions and pulled out an orb bomb from a compartment on her holster. Their only hope was if the blast took all or most of the enemy out. She stood up and stepped away from the wall to press the detonation button. Before she could activate the explosive, three laser discharges ripped through her right leg and left shoulder. The impact of the hits sent Star flying back toward the bed. She hit the floor hard and felt an explosion of pain. The orb bomb rolled harmlessly out of reach. "Star!" called Lucien.

She could feel the pain of her injuries flood every inch of her body. The agony was beyond her ability to express, even in a scream. Tears welled in Star's brown eyes and poured down into her dark brown hair. The orb bomb was their last chance and she had blown it. She failed not only a helpless child, but also the man she loved.

Then a sudden movement caught Star's eye.

She turned her head towards Lucien and Mina. Lucien's eyes were closed. Star's eyes quickly shot to his chest. To her relief, it rose and fell in shallow breaths. Mina stood next to him, but her eyes were fixed on Star. Tears streaked her little face and Star's failure to save the child broke her heart. Though she knew there was nowhere for the child to go, Star irrationally urged her to try to escape. "Mina, please! Go hide! Quick, before they come!" she begged weakly.

Mina turned back to Lucien for a moment and then to what was left of the dresser. Star saw her tiny face become pinched with determination. She moved toward the orb. *Oh no,* thought Star. *She's going to try to get the bomb.* Fear for the child's life consumed her. It took all of her strength, but she grabbed Mina's leg. "No, Mina. You'll be killed! Do as I tell you and go hide!"

The child stared down at the fallen soldier and shook her head. For the first time, Mina spoke. It was soft, like a whisper, so delicate it was barely audible over the killer laser blasts. "Trust us," she said.

Mina tried to advance, but Star had a death grip on her leg. Mina didn't struggle. She closed her eyes. When she reopened them, their violet tint seemed brighter to Star. She turned her head in the direction of the orb bomb. Blue streaks rained toward Mina, but didn't seem to touch her. Star turned her head and saw the orb bomb floating in the air. It was then Star realized Mina was much more than a telepath. The orb turned in the air. The explosive changed from yellow to brilliant blue, indicating the detonation button had somehow been pressed. Star watched with failing strength as Mina's violet eyes darted towards the dresser. The orb bomb flew to the dresser and Mina ducked down and hugged Star. The bomb exploded, causing smoke and debris to fill the room. No more laser blasts came through the entrance.

Soon after, Star could hear voices shouting her name and feet running up the stairs. She stared up at Mina in amazement. "Mina, how ... how did you know how to activate the bomb?" she asked. Mina pointed to Lucien, who had opened his eyes. Star understood that he had not been unconscious, but concentrating all his strength in directing Mina to the bomb. He smiled weakly at Star and then at Mina. "She's a brave little soldier," he whispered.

Star closed her eyes and waited to be rescued. She could feel a little hand insert itself into hers and she squeezed it.

Chapter 5 - Command Decision

"No! Not a bomb!" Osto screamed as a federation soldier tossed an orb bomb at the prison block just ahead of them. Wardon soldiers blocked their way into the prison to ensure its sole occupant did not escape. Osto had wanted to take the guards out by laser fire, so as not to risk injuring the hostage that they had come to save. The only thing he could do now was duck, and hope the orb killed only the Wardon guards outside the entrance. The carelessness of the soldier made him angry. Osto vowed that if she had sustained so much as a scratch from that bomb, he would beat him within an inch of his life.

Osto and the Pente Force team, ducked for cover before the explosion erupted. A thunderous boom emanated from the orb bomb, taking out the nearest guards and blowing a huge opening in the prison block.

The smell of blood and smoke permeated the air as they passed the bodies of Wardon soldiers that littered the floor.

Osto's first time in command of his special forces team was more difficult than he anticipated.

The Wardons had detected the rescue team almost immediately. The entire base had exploded in a flurry of laser fire almost from the moment they arrived. The Pente Force was the lead team in the rescue which made him the commander of the entire rescue mission.

Osto felt the full weight of command on his shoulders. Federation soldiers screamed into his earpiece looking for guidance, and he had to make split-second decisions. Although he gave orders with confidence and authority, he didn't like being in charge. His expertise was following orders, not giving them. He missed his Commander, Star, and wished more than anything she was leading the rescue instead of recuperating from her injuries she sustained during the Cria rescue.

Osto activated his communicator and addressed the rescue team. "Stand by, everybody. We're going in."

While Neptune stayed behind to cover their exit, she moved forward with the rest of this team through the smoke and into the now open cell area in search of the hostage. His adrenaline tempted him to be a little reckless, but his anxiety over finding his friend kept his wits intact. The smoke from the bomb made him cough and his brown eyes teary, but he didn't stop his frantic search. After a few minutes of looking into empty cells, he found her cowering in a corner cell. Osto approached and disabled the force field from the control panel on the wall. As he did so, the woman backed away as if she didn't recognize him.

She was a typical Zatokian female, tall and wafer thin. The way her long, blonde hair curved to her face made the beautiful young woman look frail.

As Osto stared down at the innocent Elaine, his anger grew at the nerve of kidnapping the sister of Queen Moreen of Zatoks and his dear friend. The Wardons had beaten her. Welts covered her bare arms and bruises had begun to form on her face. Osto's fury grew when he thought of how they must have hurt her.

The closer Osto got, the more she shook with fear. He was close enough to be recognized now but Elaina still trembled. She had known him since he first joined the Federation Chain of Life. Even in the semi-darkness of the prison, Osto looked nothing like a Wardon, and he wore a special forces uniform. Her reaction led him to conclude that her ordeal had left her traumatized.

"Elaina, it's Osto. It's okay, I'm here to take you home," he said gently as he held his hand out. Instead of taking it, Elaina shook her head spasmodically and began to cry. "No, we can't leave," she sobbed.

Osto could hear the laser fire outside the prison increase and the alarms blaring for enemy reinforcements. There was no more time. "Elaina, come on, we have to leave."

Elaina covered her face with her hands and cried harder. "No, we can't! They have the statue!"

A stray laser blast entered the prison and hit a far wall. He had no time to ask about a statue. His team was waiting for them just outside and were in increasing danger every moment they lingered. Osto yanked Elaina up by her arms and grabbed her by the waist. Throwing her over his shoulder, he carried her out of the cell as she kicked and screamed in protest.

Smoke from laser fire and orb bombs brought visibility in the prison block down to practically zero. Federation soldiers provided cover with orb bombs and laser fire. The area around the prison seemed to be filling with Wardons and Osto knew more would be coming soon. Although the rescue team was ample for the mission, the base was heavily guarded and they were in danger of being overrun.

As Osto stepped out of the prison, dragging the kicking and screaming princess behind him, he spotted the horrified expression that washed over Neptune's face. "Osto, what are you doing?"

Osto hurriedly explained his rough treatment of the princess. "She's in shock. She wouldn't come. I'll apologize later. Let's get out of here."

Still holding Elaina tightly, he and the rescue team ran from the advancing Wardons to the end of the base where the rest of the rescue team held back the enemy.

Another special forces team -- the Crimson Five -- had stayed at the entrance of the escape route with the bulk of the Federation soldiers. They had been engaging the enemy forces while Osto and his team had executed the mission. The mission had been achieved. It was time to leave the base so that it could be destroyed by Federation warships that were on the way. Osto passed Elaina off to Neptune and then walked toward the Crimson Five's commander, Marcus.

Osto knew Marcus had hard feelings about not getting command of the rescue team. He had been a special forces commander as long as his own commander and felt he deserved the assignment. Because of the Pente Force's ties to the Zatokian Royal family, however, Federation Defense had assigned the lead to the Pente Force. The two quickly shook hands. "Good work, Commander," said Marcus. Osto nodded in acknowledgement.

Suddenly, Osto heard Neptune shouting and the two men turned quickly in her direction. "Hey! Get back here! Elaina!"

Elaina had broken away from Neptune and began to go back into the enemy fire. Neptune had called after her and began to run after her. Osto realized with horror that Elaine was trying to return to the prison block. He felt a chill run up his back. "What's wrong with her?" demanded Marcus as the two raced in pursuit.

"I don't know. She's been acting crazy," answered Osto.

The two commanders ran after the two women. Neptune caught Elaina before she had gotten far. The princess fought briefly, but soon crumpled into a sobbing pile on the floor. Neptune and Osto knelt by her. Her face was tense, and her large, blue eyes flashed with urgency. "The Wardons have the Andrina Statue," she shouted hysterically.

Osto's jaw involuntarily dropped in astonishment. Now it all made sense. The Andrina Statue was important to the Zatokians. They believed that their queens are one with the planet.

Not only do they receive their power from the energy crystals that are prevalent on Zatoks, but that the material is part of their genetic make-up. When Zatokian queens die, their bodies condense into the same crystal. Andrina, one of the most powerful queens in Zatokian history, sacrificed herself to the Wardon Empire in order to save her planet. Like other queens before her, Andrina's body became a small crystal statue. More importantly, Andrina was Queen Moreen's and Elaina's mother. The stolen statue explained Elaina's behavior. Not only was it the most important symbol to her planet and a source of power for the present queen, it was also the only thing Elaina had left of her legendary mother.

Neptune hugged Elaina to her and let her cry. Neptune's voice shook with anger and her brown eyes blazed with hate. "They attacked the Zatokian temple for the statue. Elaina was just a bonus."

Elaina suddenly broke away from Neptune and grabbed Osto by the front of his uniform. Desperation clouded her eyes. "Osto, please! Let me get my mother's statue. Without it Zatoks is lost and her sacrifice would have been for nothing!"

Through her tears, Elaina told the commander the current location of the statue. Osto swore a half dozen times to vent his anger. Although the mission was to bring back the princess, the statue changed things. They couldn't let the enemy have it. He glanced around at his teammate's faces to gauge their reaction. They were outraged as well; he could see it on their faces. They would support him. He didn't even have to ask.

The battle around them continued to wage. The deafening noise from the laser fire and cannons permeated the air. More smoke billowed into the area. They didn't have a lot of time. Marcus looked around the battle and at his own team fighting. His face turned red. Osto worried that Marcus and his team may balk at the change in mission. He needed their support to get the statue back.

"Wait a minute, wait a minute," said Marcus. "I know where this is going. Osto, our mission was to bring back Elaina. Do you think we can hold the Wardons off forever?"

Osto knew he was right, but he also knew what would happen to the Zatokian monarchy if that statue was lost to the Wardons. There really wasn't any other choice.

Osto took a deep breath and looked Marcus in the eye. He was about to become a very unpopular young man. "I need you and the rescue team to make the Wardons look your way. I'm going in for the statue."

Marcus shook his head and his eyes flashed with anger. "This is a mistake. I wouldn't risk my team or yours on such a mindless stunt. I certainly wouldn't risk Elaina for a stupid crystal statue."

Osto moved in closer to Marcus. He didn't care who Marcus was, he was going through with the plan. His brown eyes locked with Marcus' grey ones. He spoke slowly and clearly so that Marcus got the full meaning of his words. "I'm the commander of this rescue team. I'm going in after that statue and you're going to cover me while I do it."

Osto could feel the anger emanating from Marcus' body. He was being challenged and Osto could tell he didn't like it. Finally, Marcus gave out a defeated sigh. He turned away from Osto and began barking orders to the rescue team. Relief momentarily flooded Osto's body. They weren't finished yet.

Osto turned to his team. "Okay guys, this has to be quick. I need everyone but Neptune to make their way back to the ship. Take Elaina with you and make sure she gets to the ship safely. Use the cannons on the Lionex to thin out the Wardons. Neptune, you're with me."

His team let out a collective, "Yes, sir," and left to carry out his orders. Osto had learned from Elaina that the statue was in the Wardon laboratory that was in the prison, which meant he had to go back to where they had just been. Osto let out a frustrated sigh. If he had listened to Elaina in the first place, they would already be heading home with both the princess and the statue. That's why Star was the commander, he thought bitterly.

Osto's gaze went back to the escape route which was quickly filling with Wardon soldiers. Anxiety rose from his stomach to his throat. They only had one chance and not much time. He took a deep breath to calm himself and signaled for Marcus to start the assault.

He heard Marcus ordered the rescue team to throw every orb they had left and to use every laser gun until all energy was drained. The commander's order resulted in a blinding flurry of weapons discharge. Cannons from the Lionex and the Crimson Five's ship, the Fantasy, began taking apart the base as they rolled forward to provide Osto and Neptune more cover. Osto and Neptune ran headlong into the Wardon soldiers that were blocking their way back into the prison.

They dodged killer streaks of blue laser fire and jumped over bodies until they reached the prison and the lab. Neptune stayed at the entrance behind some debris and fired on the few soldiers that were not occupied with the assault. Osto went inside in search of the statue. He was greeted with more enemy fire.

Only two Wardon soldiers had been left behind to guard the statue. Osto ducked behind a lab table and returned their fire. Out of the corner of his eye he saw Neptune step inside. She shot one soldier from the doorway. The other Wardon shot Neptune in the shoulder. Osto watched her fall, almost as if in slow motion. For a moment he froze in disbelief. She shouted in pain as she hit the floor hard.

A blinding rage consumed him. A white flash momentarily appeared before his eyes. In a split second he saw all the faces of his family and friends killed by the Wardon Empire. He couldn't control his left hand -- couldn't control the number of times his Ks-99 fired at the enemy soldier. Osto hit him at least a dozen times before he could regain his control and take his finger off the trigger.

The rage disappeared as fast as it had arrived. The exertion left him breathing heavy and his heart pounding. He ran back to Neptune. Everything had happened so fast. He knelt beside Neptune, who was sitting on the floor bleeding. Neptune pushed him away.

"I'm okay," she said, her voice thick with pain. The color was draining from her face. "Get the statue and let's get out of here!"

Osto nodded and left Neptune's side. He searched frantically for the statue. He found it behind a force field. He smashed the control panel and disabled the security system.

The Andrina statue was only two feet high. The detail of the image on the crystal was remarkable, as was Elaina's resemblance to her mother. Osto had never met the queen; but by just looking at the legendary statue and the fact that he too had royal Zatokian blood in his veins, he could feel her power.

There was not time to admire the statue further. He grabbed it and returned to Neptune. Blood had already saturated her beige uniform. He knew she needed medical attention. "Should I carry you?" he asked.

Neptune eyed her commander and winced. "The way you carried Elaina? No thanks. I think I'll run on my own. I may need to lean on you a bit though."

Neptune would not let him look at her wound and he worried that it was serious. He began to swear in anger, cursing the Wardons and himself for letting her get hurt. He helped her up and she leaned on him for support.

"I'm sorry, Neptune," he said.

Neptune furrowed her eyebrows. "For what? I've been shot before. It happens. Let's just get out of here."

Osto nodded and the two quickly left the lab. Enemy fire was waiting for them, but a series of explosions from the Lionex and the Fantasy caused the Wardons to turn their attention back to the rescue team.

Osto and Neptune made it back without further injury. The entire team moved out quickly. The Lionex took off moments after Osto and Neptune were on board and all the ships that carried the rescue team outran three battle cruisers sent from the Wardon home world to defend the base. The Federation Defense fleet later engaged the battle cruisers in a conflict that lasted for weeks, resulting in the destruction of the base and two of Wardon's larger ships.

On board the Lionex, Neptune's wound was bound until she got to the infirmary. To Osto's relief the laser blast hadn't severed any arteries. Osto gave the Andrina statue to Elaina, who cradled it like a precious doll until they arrived at the Federation space station on Polaris. Once there, Richard Sanderson, head of Federation Defense, and Queen Moreen greeted them.

Soon after, the grateful queen and princess returned to Zatoks. Not long after the rescue team left the Wardon base, warships from the Federation

Defense fleet arrived and engaged the battle cruisers. In a battle that lasted for weeks, Federation Defense managed to defeat the Wardon battle cruisers and destroy the base. All that didn't matter to Osto. Although there were some missteps along the way and Neptune sustained an injury that was easily treated, his mission as commander was successful.

Osto felt confident now that if the situation warranted him to head the Pente Force he could do so without worrying whether he could handle the pressure. He also knew the awesome pressure and responsibility of command and was more than happy to stand aside and let Star resume her place.

Chapter 6 - Lamia

The sour smell of formaldehyde permeated the air in the morgue on the space station of Polaris. Pia crinkled her nose as she stared at the body lying in front of her. His large brown eyes were opened in a death stare. Pia's body gave a quick, involuntarily shudder. She tried to convince herself that the freezing morgue and not the haunted expression on the soldier's face caused the spasm. The young soldier had been the fourth to be found dead in as many weeks.

She picked up the chart at the end of the table that the soldier was lying on and impatiently flipped through the file. Lt. Steve Orin received his commission only a few weeks ago. Pia tossed the file down and let out a frustrated sigh. The chart didn't mention all the similarities to this kid and the other three – young, tall, dark hair and dark eyes. "Did this one die like the others, Doctor?" she asked.

She eyed the thin, middle-aged man with a doubtful expression. The physician didn't answer her right away, but was intently examining the shirtless corpse with a medical hand scanner. She noticed that he concentrated his scan on a dark mark on the dead soldier's neck.

"He looks the same as the others," she stated impatiently.

The doctor took his eyes off his work and shot Pia

an annoyed glance. "Yes, thank you, Captain," he said curtly. "I won't be able to tell you for sure until I open him up, but it looks like the creature is responsible."

Pia raised her eyebrows. "You mean the lamia," she said.

The doctor nodded. "I'm pretty sure of it."

Pia shook her head. She didn't understand when the head of Federation Defense explained the creature to her and she certainly didn't believe it when the doctor told her. "What the hell is a lamia again and why is it coming after our soldiers?"

The doctor continued with his examination but explained to Pia again what she was up against. "A lamia was thought to be a mythical creature from medieval times. Legend has it that a lamia ate little children and young men," he said.

The doctor's introduction sparked Pia's memory. "Oh yeah, and our scientists believe they are not legendary monsters, but supposedly the real thing. They're some race of changelings that live on some remote planet on the edge of the galaxy."

"That's right. They live off the life force of humanoids, particularly young men and children, although we don't know why. And it's not my job to find out why this lamia is hunting our soldiers -- it's yours."

Pia's hazel eyes narrowed and she tossed the chart on a small table next to the body. "Fine. When you find out for sure that your monster is responsible for this kid's death, let me know."

"You still don't believe in the lamia?" he asked.

"I don't believe in fairy tales," she said as she walked away. "But Mr. Sanderson believes you and that means I have to chase after it."

Pia left the morgue and made her way to the other end of the space station to the war room where she was to meet Mr. Sanderson, head of Federation Defense. Mr. Sanderson must have considered whatever killed the soldiers a significant threat in order to leave Earth and come all the way up to the station. Pia thought there was something serious going on, but surely not some ancient imaginary creature. There wasn't any real proof that the planet the creatures lived on really existed. *Oh well*, she thought. *I don't have to believe in it, I just have to hunt it down and kill it.*

From behind her, Pia could hear fast approaching footsteps. She turned to see her boyfriend and fellow Special Forces soldier, Ronan, trying to catch up with her. She didn't stop walking – Mr. Sanderson wanted to hear about the dead soldier – but she did slow her pace so that he was by her side within moments.

"Find out anything?" he asked.

"Yeah, it's almost certain that what killed the other three killed this one too," she said.

"It's too bad that Star and the others are on other assignments," he stated.

Pia stopped and shot Ronan an angry glare at the mention of her commander and teammates. "Are you saying that I can't handle this on my own?" she demanded.

Ronan grabbed her arm. Surprise washed over her face as her eyes went from the hand on her arm to the owner. Concern clouded his brown eyes. "Pia, I'm worried about this assignment. This thing is dangerous. You're a capable soldier to be sure, but any one of us would need backup on this. You don't know what this thing is capable of."

Pia continued to glare at Ronan for a moment longer, then wrestled her arm out of his grip and began to walk away. "If Mr. Sanderson didn't think I could handle it, he would have given this to your team. I've got it covered."

Ronan followed her down the well-lit hallway at a safe distance. "Let me back you up. My assignment sheet is clear. I'd feel a lot better if you had another gun on this mission."

"My back doesn't need guarding," she huffed.

"How are you planning to kill this thing? Do you even know what it looks like?"

Pia picked up her pace, hoping that Ronan would get the hint not to continue to follow her. "That's my problem," she said coolly. "Oh, and thanks for your vote of confidence in my ability."

Ronan stopped following her just as she got to the War Room door. She looked over her shoulder to see him watching her with the same concerned expression. Before Ronan could protest more, Pia disappeared through the door.

***

The spacious war room was filled with 3D charts of every system in the Federation lining the walls and communications screens hanging from the ceiling. Pia made her way to the center of the room where Mr. Sanderson sat alone at the head of a large rectangular table. She saluted him and waited for the leader of Federation Defense to address her. He motioned for her to sit down. "It was the lamia?" he asked in his smooth British accent.

"It sure looks like it," she answered as she plopped down in one of the cushy chairs.

Mr. Sanderson glanced at the soldier over his glasses with an annoyed expression on his face. "Pia, we've just had an intelligence report from your teammate Neptune. She was able to download information from the central computer of a Wardon battlecruiser that she recently was assigned to destroy. There really is a lamia and a Wardon soldier is holding its leash. It's here to kill Osto and Nine," he said.

Sanderson pushed some papers in front of Pia, who quickly read them. The information sparked Pia's anger. "Well, Tozar really is an idiot," she said irritably. "But the guys aren't even here."

The Wardon Empire, particularly their Emperor Tozar, considered Pia and the Pente Force a significant threat. He would use any unconventional methods in his attempt to assassinate them.

"Apparently, he doesn't know that," Mr. Sanderson said. "The last intelligence he received must have placed the boys at this base."

Pia furrowed her eyebrows. "But that doesn't even make sense. Tozar knows what Osto and Nine look like. Why have the monster kill the other soldiers?"

"Apparently, lamias are not the smartest creatures. She's hungry and has to feed on something. She's been pretty close to her target. All of those young men who have been killed fit the description of Osto and Nine."

Mr. Sanderson pressed a button in front of him. A hologram of a scaly, serpent-like biped creature about five and a half feet tall appeared on the table. Pia slowly rose from her chair and stared at the snarling beast in awe. "Neptune also found this among the files. They are real, Pia. This is a lamia."

Pia circled the table, taking in the hideous creature as Mr. Sanderson continued. "She can take the shape of a beautiful young woman to lure young men to her."

Mr. Sanderson pressed another button to show the lamia transform into a beautiful blonde girl of around 20. "This is the form she takes. She pretends to be in trouble and when a gullible young man gets close enough, she hypnotizes them. At that point, she either leads or carries him off to her nest to feed."

Pia felt her blood run cold. Nine and Osto would fall for the deception. The leader of Federal Defense pressed another button showing a lamia in action. Pia watched in horror as the creature hypnotized a victim with a mere glance and then led him away. It only took a moment for her to do it and the victim didn't put up a struggle. The creature then led the young man to a cave and began feeding by sucking blood from the victim's neck. "So this thing is like a vampire?" asked Pia, disgusted with the scene playing out in front of her.

"No. First, lamias are real and Terran vampires

are legend. They can travel in the day and are not affected by any of the legendary weapons such as garlic or holy water. However, they do possess incredible strength, and their sharp teeth and claws are as dangerous as any wild animal that exists in the Federation."

To Pia's relief, Mr. Sanderson stopped the simulation and she sat back down. "Does Wardon have any more of these things running around the Federation?" she asked.

"Not that we know of. We believe through the intelligence we received that they are using this method of attack as an experiment. If she proves to be successful, then they could try to bring more lamias up from the planet. Fortunately, we have a battle cruiser on its way to take the planet to make sure nothing comes up from the surface."

"Okay, so I'll get rid of both the Wardon and the lamia," said Pia matter-of-factly. She hoped that her voice portrayed her as being more certain than she really was.

"What's your plan?" asked Mr. Sanderson.

"Well, based on what you just gave me, her current pattern is that she feeds once a week. The victims were all last seen alive at the night club just on the edge of the base. They all disappeared on Saturday nights. Today is Friday, so tomorrow I will go down there and hunt her down. The Wardon can't be seen in the club, so he'll be outside somewhere waiting for her. Now that I know what I'm looking for, I'm sure I won't have a hard time tracking the scum down. Once I have him, I'll hit the club and wait for the lamia to pick her next meal."

Mr. Sanderson let out a long, audible breath. "You have to be very careful, Pia. You'll have a weapon, but she's still very dangerous. I don't want another soldier lying in the morgue."

Pia straightened in her chair. "I'm always careful," she said.

Mr. Sanderson took off his glasses and began to clean them. "No you're not. But you do get the job done. Dismissed," he said without looking up. Pia saluted and left to prepare.

***

On Saturday evening, a Wardon wearing Terran clothing scurried down an alleyway near the Officer's Club. Pia didn't have a problem finding him. She was used to hunting Wardons; she had been doing it for most of her life and could pick one out as easily as she could pick out a fighter ship from a battle cruiser. She gave out an annoyed sigh as she followed the enemy from a distance. *This is too easy*, she thought.

Pia followed the Wardon out of the alley and into an empty street. Pia, dressed in street clothes, checked up and down the deserted way before hurrying to catch up with the Wardon. When she was only a few yards away, she called to the soldier in Wardonese. "Where are you going in such a hurry?" she demanded.

The Wardon stopped short. Pia guessed that it was more because she used his native tongue than the question. Pia smiled to herself. Although he didn't turn around, she knew he was scared – she could almost smell it. She gripped her Ks-99 laser tightly in her hand, anticipating any sudden moves the enemy might make. After a few moments went by without any sort of response or movement from the Wardon, Pia called to him again. "I am looking for the lamia. Where is it?"

"I don't know what you're talking about," said the Wardon without turning around.

Well, there's a surprise, she thought.

Just as she was about to order the Wardon to turn around and face her, someone came out from the side street. Although she couldn't see who it was, she knew the voice that echoed through the night towards the Wardon.

It was Ronan.

"Stop right there!" he shouted.

His proximity was closer to the Wardon than hers and his voice startled the enemy. The Wardon pulled out a weapon and pointed it at Ronan. Pia saw the weapon go up, and before the Wardon could squeeze the trigger, she fired. Pia's aim was dead on and the Wardon dropped where he stood.

Pia ran to the Wardon, but Ronan got to him first. "Don't touch him!" she yelled.

Ronan quickly stood up from the body. As Pia neared them, she could feel her face flush. She was even angrier when she saw that Ronan was dressed in a Pente Force uniform. "What the hell do you think you're doing?" she demanded.

"I was trying to help you!"

Pia searched the Wardon's body. He was most

definitely dead and he carried no intelligence. "Help me? Are you kidding?" she said as she kicked the dead Wardon. "You call this helping me? And what are you doing in our uniform?"

"I was going to pretend to be Nine and catch the lamia. I was heading to the club when I saw you trailing the Wardon."

Pia put her weapon in her holster. Images of the lamia feeding flashed through her mind. "Are you crazy? You wouldn't be able to defend yourself against her," she said.

She looked down at the dead Wardon and let out an angry breath. "Look what you've done! I was going to use him to lure her here. You've just made my job that much harder."

"Use me, what's the problem?" asked Ronan. "I mean, you're sure that killing her isn't going to be hard, so I wouldn't be in any danger, right?"

Pia heard the challenge in his tone. Ronan shared the same characteristics as her male teammates. She was tempted to use him – he would be perfect – but a flash of the lamia eating her victim returned. No, she was not going to risk him. "I don't need your help. I don't want your help. Go back to your quarters and take off that uniform."

Ronan opened his mouth to say something, but Pia turned her back on him and walked away.

***

Pia entered the crowded, smoky nightclub. She pushed through the mass of people gyrating to the deafening music. Keeping the image of the beautiful blonde girl from the video in her head, she squinted through the hazy smoke trying to locate the lamia. In just a short time of study, Pia felt that she knew her routine. The fact that the Wardon was lurking outside the club enforced her theory that the lamia would strike tonight.

The Special Forces officer waded through the crowd, the thumping vibration of the music resonating in her ears. Suddenly, a very drunk young man stopped her and asked her to dance. She was about to decline politely when a figure over the man's shoulder caught her eye.

She saw the lamia.

Worse yet, the lamia had a young man by the hand and was leading him out of the club. Pia felt a chill rise up her spine when she made out the Pente Force uniform and the familiar face – Ronan's face.

She swore under her breath and tried to go after them, but the drunken soldier grabbed her arm in an effort to get her to dance. Pia felt her panic let go on the young man as she punched him in the stomach to get him to release her. Free from the drunk's grip, Pia tried to make a quick exit from the club, but the tangle of arms and legs dancing to the impossibly loud music hampered her efforts considerably.

After what seemed like hours, she arrived at the door. She didn't have to wonder where the lamia was taking Ronan. She would go and find her master in the alley and then feed.

Cautiously she raced back to the alley with her weapon in hand. Pia's eyes quickly adjusted to the dim light. For a while, all she heard were the far way noises of traffic and people. As she walked down the alley, she noticed that the body of the Wardon was now propped up in a sitting position. The lamia must be close.

Suddenly, the silence gave way to the sounds of a struggle further down the alley. Pia began to run towards the noise but then slowed to a quick walk, as the way became nearly pitch black. She listened intently for any noise that would give away the lamia's exact location. And then she heard it almost right in front of her in the shadows.

"No."

The protest seemed more like a weak moan than a strong command, but Pia knew the voice to be Ronan's. She aimed her weapon towards the shadows. "Get off of him!" she demanded.

Momentary panic rose in her. The vision of the victim's face in the war room was now replaced with Ronan's. She tried to focus her attention on the angry hiss that emanated from the shadows. Pia peered toward the direction of the sound. What suddenly leapt out at her was not the beautiful blond woman, but a hideous, scaly creature. This more than anything caught her off-guard. The force of the attack caused Pia to drop her weapon.

The lamia swung at Pia, its fist connecting with her ribcage. The air rushed from Pia's lungs as she momentarily doubled over. The lamia had considerable strength, but so did Pia. She fought the pain in her side and wedged her shoulder into the monster's stomach, ramming the creature into the wall. The effort paid off – the lamia struggled for breath.

Although winded, the lamia charged wildly at Pia again. She sidestepped the serpent creature at the last moment, nearly sending it hurtling against the alley wall. The lamia's red eyes flashed as it roared in outrage. It came back at Pia, who gave out her own war cry as the two locked arms. The two wrestled in an attempt to get the superior position. The pain in Pia's side became unbearable and it didn't take long for the lamia to get the upper hand. The lamia caught Pia off-balance and whipped her across the alley and into the wall. Her back and head hit the wall hard and the wind was once again knocked out of her. She felt her knees buckle as she slid down the wall. Pia could see victory in the lamia's twisted face as it charged again for what they both knew would be the last time.

She had failed. She had underestimated her opponent and overestimated her own abilities. Now she and Ronan would have to pay for her mistake with their lives.

Suddenly, Pia heard something scraping across the ground. She saw a laser slide from the shadows, across the alley toward her hand. The creature roared at the sound and whirled around to see where it came from. This was her chance. Pia took up the weapon and fired at the lamia. She hit the creature between the eyes. Shock spread over the lamia's face as a thin trail of blood trickled down where the laser bolt entered. The monster dropped dead to the ground.

Pia tried to get up, but the pain in her side made it impossible. Instead, she crawled in the direction of where the weapon had come.

Ronan was propped up against the wall on the other side of the alley. He was panting and blood trickled down his neck and stained his uniform.

"I... told... you... back up...," he managed before he passed out.

Pia checked to make sure he was breathing. She activated her communicator and radioed for help.

***

Both Special Forces soldiers were transported to the base infirmary. Pia received two cracked ribs as a result of her run-in with the lamia. Though he lost a considerable amount of blood, to Pia's relief, Ronan would survive.

She crept into Ronan's room to see if he was sleeping, and his eyes opened the moment she closed the door behind her. "How do you feel?" she asked.

"I feel pretty foolish." he said. "You were right. There was no way I could stop her. I've never felt so helpless and stupid in my life."

"We were both wrong, let's just leave it at that," she said as she gave him a kiss before leaving. "I'm just glad you're okay."

"I'm glad we're both okay," he replied.

Pia gave him a sly grin. "I had it all covered," she said with a wink as she slipped out the door.

Chapter 7 - A Withering Force

Nine felt a hand grab the crook of his right arm and jerk it. He turned to find his friend Dr. Jared Thomas in a bloodstained lab coat trying to examine the wound on the right side of his head. Blood from the injury he sustained during the Wardon attack trickled from his head down to his neck. In all the noise and confusion, he had forgotten about it.

"You better let me clean that up for you," said Dr. Jared Thomas as he pulled out a bottle of antiseptic from his lab coat. Nine winced at the thought of the solution cleaning his wound and stinging more than the original wound. Nine brushed his friend aside as he turned back to the war zone.

"No thanks. I just came to drop off a wounded soldier. She needs your attention more than I do," he said.

"Nine, come back! I need to see your head!" shouted Jared.

Nine ignored the command. His thoughts turned back to the argument that he and his commander had before he had left the war zone with the soldier. He had wanted someone else to bring her back so that he could stay with the team. Star had wanted a medic to look at his head. Nine had argued that she was treating him like a child. Star had concluded the argument by ordering him, at the top of her lungs, to get back to the safe zone and have his wound checked.

As Nine began to head back to his team, he heard a frantic voice resonate from the receiver in his ear.

"Nine, Wardon's have taken over the main corridor. We've been cut off. We're in Hangar Bay 6. Bring help!"

A chill went through his body. The voice belonged to Star.

"How? They weren't even close when I left," he asked.

He heard laser fire and shouts from his other teammates in the background. How did the enemy get so far so fast?

"We're being ambushed! Bring reinforcements!" shouted Star.

Nine had already started running to the Command Center adjacent to the war torn base. "I'm on my way!" he said breathlessly.

The laser fire and shouts continued in his ear. Nine could feel his heart trying to pound out of his chest. Anxiety rose from the pit of his stomach as he pictured in his mind what was happening. The simple mission of routing out some Wardon platoons from a Federation Chain of Life Base had become a full-on battle with an army. It had turned out to be a much larger Wardon invasion force than was originally thought. Federation Defense troops were struggling to defend the base. More Federation Defense troops were coming, but Nine wondered if it would be too late. He had to get help; he had to find Charlie Baker. As he neared the Command Center, more shouts came from the receiver.

"We can't get out. They're too many of them. Wait, what's that stuff they're ..."

Star began to cough in Nine's ear. He stopped short in front of the Command Center, frozen with fear.

"Star?"

Star continued coughing. "Get away from the gas," he heard her shout at someone. "Nine, stay away from the gas! Stay away ..."

After another fit of coughing, the transmission died. Nine tried frantically to reestablish contact, but no one responded. Oh God, he thought, they're dead.

He ran into the Command Center to find Charlie. He found him in the back, monitoring the security cameras and calling the Wardon's positions into the Federation Knight Battalion Commanders. Charlie commanded the Federation Knight portion of the Federation Army and was a long-time friend of the team.

Nine's quick movement into the room caught Charlie's attention. A tired expression instantly changed to one of concern. "Nine, what are you doing here?"

Nine quickly made his way to Charlie's side and scanned the half dozen monitors in front of them. When he didn't find what he was looking for, he turned to Charlie. "Punch up Hangar 6," he ordered.

Confusion shadowed Charlie's face. Nine saw his eyes go to his head injury. "Why?"

"Just do it!"

Nine could feel himself losing control. He needed to see what had happened to his team before he and whoever he could get to come with him went headlong into a Wardon ambush. Charlie punched the command into the computer and brought up a gruesome scene. Nine lost all feeling in his body. His teammates were sprawled out on the floor. A white mist had begun to lift from the hangar. Wardon chemical warfare. The color drained from Charlie's face. "Oh no," he said.

Nine caught a movement from the corner of the screen and hit the toggle command on the computer. The security camera followed a company of gas mask-wearing Wardons exiting and sealing the entrance to the hangar behind them. Nine heard a flurry of reports coming in from the Federation Knights. Apparently, the invasion force had taken the entire left wing of the base in a matter of minutes.

"Nine, what happened?" asked Charlie, his grey eyes fixed on the monitor.

Nine toggled the security camera back to his team and focused on his commander. "We rescued an injured Knight from the left wing. I brought her to medical," he said as he pulled the camera in for a close-up of Star's chest. "I didn't want to go. Star ordered me to. I was only gone a few minutes!"

Nine struck a nearby wall in frustration as he and Charlie studied the monitor and waited. To Nine's relief, Star's chest rose and fell. They were still alive.

"We need to get a team together. Coming?" asked Nine.

Charlie nodded and started to follow Nine out the door. He turned to the monitor that was fixed on the hangar. He suddenly stopped short. Nine impatiently turned around.

"What?" Nine asked angrily.

Charlie's eyebrows furrowed. He pointed at the monitor. "Star's face."

Nine returned to the screen and felt another chill go through him. Star's face seemed sunken. Before his eyes, her skin began to wrinkle. Nine quickly moved the camera around to the other members of the team. It was happening to all of them. Nine bolted from the Command Center, pulling Charlie with him. Charlie called another soldier in to warn the battalion commanders of chemical warfare and to monitor the security cameras. He also called a couple of platoons from the back lines to assist with the rescue. The Pente Force were well thought of and respected. There weren't many Knights that wouldn't do what they could to help save them.

Nine called three medics to accompany them with emergency medical kits, including Jared.

Nine knew the chemical the Wardon's attacked his team with and what was happening to them as a result. Federation Defense termed the chemical "withering juice." The wrinkling or "withering" resulted from a severe allergic reaction to being exposed to the chemical. Eventually, the windpipe closes, suffocating the victim. The Pente Force's genetics were Zatokian and Terran. No one knew if the chemical would affect them.

Until now. Nine's anger rose. *The Wardons get*

a real kick out of watching our soldiers die like that, he thought. Chemical warfare was one of Lord Tozar's favorite means of killing his enemies.

Fortunately for the team, Jared and his team of scientists had found an antidote six months ago. They could be treated if they were reached in time. The Wardon scientists were creative with their chemical toys, but not very bright. Nine knew the antidote would save them if he could get through to the hangar.

With his heart racing, Nine hopped into the driver's seat of an armed transport and activated the controls. Charlie rode shotgun. The medics sat in the back of the ten-man transport and prepared for their future patients. A young soldier hopped on the back of the armored vehicle. Forty Federation Knights followed behind the transport armed with KS-25 laser rifles, chemical orb bombs, and battle armor.

The Federation Knights clanked awkwardly in their stiff, bulky light gray armor as they tried to fire their weapons at the increasing amount of enemy soldiers and keep up with the transport. Nine tried to be patient, keeping the speed of the vehicle to a point where the Knights could keep up, but his anxiety to get to the team sometimes made his foot a little too heavy on the acceleration pedal.

The Federation base, remotely located on the moon of Zenora, served as part of the early warning detection system that identified Wardon ships entering zones occupied by the Federation Chain of Life. It also had the dual purpose of a refueling station for Federation fleet ships. Despite its importance, the base was relatively small. The facility consisted mostly of communications rooms and hangars connected with wide, well-lit corridors.

Smoke now filled those corridors and made visibility in them poor. As the transport left the Green Zone, Nine could see an increase of bodies of both Federation Knights and Wardon soldiers littering the floor. Noise came from all around. He tried to block out the chaos of the yelling, both in English and Wardonese, mixed with laser cannons firing and bombs exploding so he could concentrate on his mission.

The sounds of laser fire and cannons increased as they went deeper into the Wardon-occupied portion of the base. The stench of orb bombs and burnt flesh filled Nine's nostrils, causing him to cough.

The smell of war usually got Nine's adrenaline pumping, but now it filled him with anxiety. He thought of his fight with Star. They had argued many times before, but now it seemed as though he would never get a chance to tell her he was sorry.

To Nine's relief, the rescue team began to advance at a faster pace. The Federation Knights were now in front of the transport, firing at the enemy in an attempt to get to Hangar Bay 6. Blue streaks of laser fire bounced off the Federation Knights. The cannon in the back of the transport fired wildly, and the soldier operating the cannon howled with delight each time he hit a Wardon. Nine longed to be up on the cannon firing at the enemy to punish them all for what they had done. He knew driving the transport to the hangar was a priority.

As Nine sat behind the wheel of the transport the images of his withering teammates haunted him. He could feel the panic rising within him. The transport wasn't going fast enough. He would never reach them in time. Helpless, Nine punched the steering mechanism of the transport in frustration.

"Calm down!" shouted Charlie.

"This is nuts! They'll be raisins before we get there!"

"It's just down the hall, Nine. We'll make it."

Charlie rubbed his temples and let out an audible, shaky breath. Nine realized that Charlie was just as anxious as he was to get to their friends. Nine tried to relax a little. "You're right. They're tough. They'll wait for us," he said, trying to make them both feel better.

The rescue team continued to push through the gauntlet of enemy laser fire. As they moved forward, more Federation Knights came in from different areas of the base. They followed the transport and began to rid that portion of the base of Wardon soldiers.

Just as they reached the sealed hangar door an explosion hit the back of the armed transport, blowing the back tires and killing half a dozen Federation Knights. Nine swore furiously as he hopped out of the vehicle wielding his Ks-99. The corridor to the hangar was wide and Wardon soldiers were firing at them from both sides. The bomb could have come from anywhere. The heavy smoke stung Nine's eyes, but he began to fire wildly in the direction of where he thought the Wardon soldiers were. The smoke from the volume of weapons discharge hung like a fog. He couldn't see past the transport.

Nine realized the laser cannon on the transport went silent. He looked to the back of the vehicle and found the enthusiastic young soldier slumped dead over his precious cannon. Nine took a moment to grieve for the soldier. He didn't know him, but Nine respected the way he fought against his enemy.

Charlie called to him from the hangar door. Before he joined Charlie, Nine flung an orb bomb through the smoke in the direction of the blue streaks of laser fire directed at the transport. The Federation Knights continued to fire as some of their colleagues attempted to repair the back end of the transport. Jared and the medics had also left the vehicle and waited with Charlie by the door of the hangar.

As Nine approached the hangar door, he heard Charlie swear incessantly and bang his fist against the controls. The door stood between Nine and his teammates. Luckily for them, there wasn't a Wardon lock he couldn't pick. Nine pushed Charlie out of the way and fired his Ks-99 at the control panel. He stuck his hands inside the smoking hole and began to connect the wires to the lock. He then reattached the loose power cable to the controls and unsealed the door.

Nine, Charlie, Jared and the medics put on their own gas masks and rushed into the hangar while the rest of the rescue team repaired the transport and held off the Wardons. Nine went to his commander. Star's condition seemed grave. If it weren't for her commander's patch, he wouldn't have recognized her. Star's labored breathing resulted in short rasps. Nine turned to Jared, who already had a needle in her arm administering the antidote. To his relief, the other medics were doing the same to the rest of his teammates.

Nine scooped Star up in his arms and began to carry her back to the transport. Charlie took Neptune, Jared had Pia and the other medics had Osto. Suddenly another bomb shook the base. It detonated close to the transport, barely missing it.

Before Nine could put Star down, Charlie had already handed Neptune off to another Knight. He jumped on the back of the transport, lifted the dead soldier off the cannon and started to fire.

Nine, Jared and the other medics quickly loaded the team into the transport. Charlie kept firing the laser cannon while the Federation Knights continued to change the back tires. Fear for Charlie enveloped Nine -- he wasn't wearing battle armor.

"Charlie, get down! You're gonna get killed!" he shouted as he fired his Ks-99 into the smoke. Charlie didn't look from his task.

"Get to the wheel! We've gotta get out of here as soon as those wheels are replaced. I'll come down when we're ready to move!"

Nine cursed Charlie a dozen times as he jumped into the transport. Five minutes later, Nine heard someone bang on the back of the transport. Nine started the vehicle and called for Charlie to get in. Charlie climbed into the seat beside him. Nine heard his heavy breathing and thought it was the exertion of operating the cannon. Only when Nine turned to back up the transport did he see that the left side of Charlie's uniform was stained with blood. Nine could feel the color draining from his face.

"It's not bad," said Charlie as he winced in pain.

Nine didn't try to hide his irritation. "Yeah, sure. Next time when I tell you to get down, do it. Jared!"

Jared helped Charlie to the back of the transport and began treating him. Nine turned the vehicle around and headed back to safer territory. As he did, he heard an armored Knight jump on to operate the cannon. Nine thought of the dead soldier and said a quick prayer that his replacement wouldn't join him in the afterworld.

***

Going back the way they came was far from easy, but it was a lot quicker than when they came in. The Federation Army had gained quite a bit of ground since they had left. There weren't as many Wardon soldiers firing at them. One of the medics came to the front of the transport and reported that the team was responding well to the treatment. Their Zatokian genes were helping them to regenerate at an accelerated rate, but they were still in serious condition. Charlie's injuries required stitches, but to Nine's relief, no arteries were severed and he would recover.

Nine felt an inner calm take over. Everyone had made it through this time. He and Star would be able to argue again. He heard the laser cannon on the back of the transport fire and he smiled.

Chapter 8 - Rescue on Daria

Star rested in a wooded area on planet Daria after crash landing her two-person "Falcon" fighter. Six hours before, she and one of her Pente Force teammates, Pia, had been part of an attack force fighting the Wardon Empire near Daria's first moon.

She had landed the fighter without benefit of landing gear. It had slid sideways through a clearing, plowing through a group of trees, before finally skidding to a halt. The crash had shattered glass and destroyed the ship's front and rear thrusters and had ruptured the fuel tank. The two women were forced to leave the fighter for fear of an explosion. Before leaving, Star tried to call her four other teammates for help, but the radio in the fighter was destroyed. She tried to call on her wrist communicator, but no one replied.

Star hurt all over. Cuts and bruises covered her face and body. To her relief, Pia, who had been seated in the back, had only sustained a few scratches. She had gone off to a nearby cave to see if they could use it for shelter for the night.

Suddenly, Star heard the noises of branches snapping and someone running. She immediately thought of her friend. Stiff from her wounds, she managed to get up to investigate. With her Ks-99 laser in her hand, she stepped out of the trees onto a game trail.

Star's concern grew as the running sounds got closer. Then Pia ran straight for her with hazel green eyes wide with fear. An animal about eight feet tall, covered with long, brown hair running on two legs began closing in on Pia. The thing's pointy ears were flattened onto its head and sharp teeth flashed in murderous rage. Its blue eyes seemed too big for its face. As it ran, the creature's long arms swung wildly, giving it a surreal, maniacal appearance.

Star got into an attack position as quickly as her stiff muscles would move. Pia was only a few yards from Star when she slipped and fell on some leaves and hurled forward onto her stomach. With the animal in clear sight, Star fired her weapon. The creature gave a short cry and fell dead. Star let out a painful groan once the threat was eliminated. Every muscle in her bruised body screamed in protest.

Pia rolled from her stomach onto her back to survey the dead animal. "God, that was close!"

Star let out an angry sigh and painfully placed her weapon in her holster. "Where's your laser?" she demanded.

Pia got up from the ground and attempted to brush the dirt from her beige special forces uniform. "It flew out of my hand when that thing jumped out at me and grabbed my arm. I swear I never heard it coming. It took me completely by surprise. And that face! Star, I've never seen anything like it."

Star looked at the animal's body and wondered what else was out there. "Pia, we have to find that weapon. Without it, we only have mine. Who knows how many of those creatures are out here."

Pia nodded, her eyes clouded. "I'll go get it. It fell somewhere in the woods."

Star shook her head. The image of the attacking monster played once more in her mind. "We'll go together," she said.

Pia silently turned and started for the fighter. Star walked slightly behind her teammate. Her muscles screamed with every step, but her mind was not on her wounds. Wardons were swarming above them in the stratosphere, and the rest of the team was up there without her. They needed to make contact with the rest of the team and get off the planet as soon as possible. As they walked, Star observed the area. It teemed with rainbow colored flowers and vegetation. Mountains stretched to the horizon, meeting a blue sky. She could hear birds chirping softly in the thin, tall trees that smelled something like pine. This place is beautiful, she thought -- and dangerous. If that animal was any indication of the ferocity of the wildlife on the planet, the sooner they left the better.

It wasn't long before they reached the wreckage. Pia picked up her Ks-99 from the ground. Star heard the sound of branches breaking ahead of them. Her body stiffened as she thought of the possibility of facing another creature. She took out her weapon and signaled Pia to follow her behind a large tree a few feet away.

Four armed Wardon soldiers came into the clearing. They were short, gray-skinned humanoids with bushy v-shaped eyebrows. Two soldiers checked the wreckage and reported to the others that there were no bodies inside. Out of the corner of her eye, Star saw Pia aim her weapon at one of the soldiers. Star took in a quick breath as she realized Pia was about to put them in danger. She grabbed Pia's arm and shook her head no. Pia furrowed her eyebrows but made no move to disobey her commander.

After a few minutes, the Wardon soldiers began heading back into the forest. When they disappeared from sight, Pia turned to Star and began her protest.

"There were only four! We could've taken them," she whispered angrily.

"No, there may be more out there," said Star.

Now, more than ever, they needed to get off Daria. She wanted to fight the Wardons as much as Pia, but she knew her injuries would hinder them. If they revealed themselves for a fight, it would cost them dearly if there were more soldiers. Two Ks-99s would not stand against an army of Wardons.

Star worried about her other teammates. If the Wardons sent a ship to hunt for them, they could not be worried about using every available man for the fight taking place in the stars. Had the enemy won the battle? What happened to the team? Star pressed a button on her wrist communicator, hoping to reach the rest of her team.

"This is Star. Can anyone hear me?" After a moment, a voice cracked in her earpiece. It was Nine.

"Star? Where are you?" he said.

Relief flowed over Star. "We're on Daria. The falcon's wrecked. You have to come get us. What's going on up there? There are Wardon soldiers wandering around down here looking for us."

"I don't know. From where I'm sitting, they can't spare anyone. The <u>Black Widow</u> destroyed their battle cruiser. The fight took us all the way to the fifth moon. There are still some enemy ships, but our fighters are more or less cleaning up after the <u>Black Widow</u>. I'll let the general know we're coming to get you. It'll take us a while before we can get there. I'll lock onto your homing frequency for a location when we get close enough."

"See you in a while," she said and signed off. The Wardons' presence on Daria still puzzled her. She decided it might be a good idea to find out how many Wardons were around the planet. The general would want to send a team down.

Star started to walk in the direction the Wardon soldiers had gone. Pia stood in front of her and raised her eyebrows.

"We're going after them?" she asked hopefully.

"We have a while before the team gets here. I'd rather have the enemy in my sights until then," answered Star as they headed into the forest.

***

Star and Pia followed the Wardons through the trees and brush, being careful not to follow too close. After about 15 minutes they came to a clearing. Star stopped short. She felt a cold chill go up her spine. Another Federation Defense ship, a one-person "Hawk," lay sprawled out in the tall grass. The Wardons walked past the wreckage without checking for a body.

"They've already been here," whispered Pia. Her comment mirrored Star's uneasy thoughts. When the Wardons disappeared into the forest, they checked the fighter for a body and found nothing. The pilot had probably followed them to Daria to help. But a one-person fighter? Star's mind raced. Who would be crazy enough to attempt a rescue in such a small ship? One thing was for sure -- whoever it was, the Wardons had him or her.

She thought of the pilot in the hands of the enemy. Forty-five minutes was a long time to be in Wardon hands. Too long. Star decided they couldn't wait for back up. Her injuries would hinder their efforts, so they would have to keep surprise on their side. It was the only chance they had. She turned to Pia who gave her a mischievous grin. Star knew she couldn't wait to plunge into another fight with the Wardon Empire. "What's the plan?" asked Pia anxiously.

Star's gaze went to the area where the Wardons disappeared. "Follow them back to camp. Then we'll see."

They followed the Wardons for another ten minutes until they reached their camp. Star left Pia behind a large boulder, and then moved in closer for a better look. She crouched down and surveyed the area. She saw a ship that appeared to be damaged. She could see the burn marks of the laser cannons, probably made by a fairly large ship from Federation Defense. Star guessed that the Wardon's ship had also crashed. They probably found the soldier and were thinking to take him back to their battle cruiser to torture him. Star couldn't help but grin at the fact that their battle cruiser no longer existed.

Her grin faded when she spotted the soldier. He was laying on the ground, unconscious and facing away from her. She moved to another tree to get a better look. Star could tell by his dark blue uniform that he was a member of the Federation Force Police (FFP), but couldn't see the markings to determine his rank.

As Star strained to see the soldier's face, a Wardon began kicking him in the ribs. Finally, the Wardon kicked him with such force, the FFP flipped over to his stomach, causing his head to turn in Star's direction.

Star took in a quick breath and her eyes went wide. Star knew that face. It was Charlie Baker, commander of the FFP's and her long-time friend. Suddenly, it all made sense to her. Charlie and his unit were also part of the battle. He couldn't sit back knowing she was in danger. He came to save her. The ever-gallant Charlie to the rescue. Now who had to rescue whom? Panic overtook her for a moment. She wanted to run in and shoot up the camp, but she knew she couldn't. The pain from her injuries shot through her with increasing intensity. Both she and Charlie required medical attention as soon as possible. She needed a plan and she needed one quickly, but she found it hard to concentrate as she watched the Wardon continue to kick Charlie.

Suddenly, an animal like the one that attacked Pia stormed into the camp and pounced on one of the Wardon soldiers. It began to claw its victim, but the Wardon had excellent reflexes and pushed the animal off. The animal began to wail in a high-pitched screech as it picked itself up. The Wardon scrambled to reach a gun. The other Wardon soldier left Charlie to assist the others in killing the beast. The attack reminded her of how easily Wardons could be distracted. A plan popped into Star's head. She limped back to Pia.

The pain increased with every step and she hoped she would have the strength to execute her part of the plan. When she reached Pia, she was practically out of breath. "It's Charlie. They've got Charlie," she said to her teammate in quick, painful breaths.

Pia's eyes widened and she let out an audible breath. "Oh God, Star!"

"I have a plan to save him. I need you to a play 'bird with a broken wing.'"

Pia immediately regained her composure and nodded. She bent down to rip the pant leg of her uniform. She took a knife out of a pouch on her holster and scraped it against her bare leg, bloodying herself enough to make a convincing wound. Then, she took her Ks-99 and stuffed it in her boot. "Ready," she said confidently.

"I don't know how many will follow you, but you'll have to take them out on your own. You'll have plenty of cover if you attack in the forest. I'll deal with the ones that stay with Charlie," said Star as she checked the energy level of her weapon. Pia flashed her commander a confident look. "This will be a piece of cake," she said.

Star looked up from her weapon and pointed a finger at the young woman. "Don't fool around, Pia. Just take care of them and come back. I'm really hurting and I might need your help," she said sternly. "Wait for me to circle around, and then come out."

Pia replaced her confidence with a more serious expression as Star turned to get into position.

* * *

When Star got behind a tree close to Charlie, she signaled Pia to begin her attack. Moments later, Pia shuffled out of the trees gripping her injured leg and moaning. Star couldn't help but give out a disgusted sigh. Pia was over exaggerating – Star thought she sounded like a dying cow. However, she got the soldier's attention. She put on a frightened look and let out an overacted scream, then shuffled back into the trees and disappeared. The Wardons scrambled to their feet and grabbed their weapons. Four followed Pia into the woods, leaving three for Star.

Star moved behind their ship, only a few feet from the remaining soldiers. They were still staring into the woods where the others had followed Pia. Suddenly, sounds of laser fire and a male voice screaming saturated the air. Two of the remaining Wardons began to move toward the forest.

Surprise was on Star's side and she took advantage of it. She stepped out from behind the shuttle and shot the soldier nearest to the forest. Before the other two could react, she killed the second soldier. The third fired his weapon. Star tried to jump out of the way, but her reflexes were off due to her injuries. The Wardon's blast struck her in the leg. As she fell, she held up her Ks-99 and fired. Only by pure luck did she hit the Wardon in the chest and kill him. Star let out a groan and clutched at her bloody leg for a moment. Pain seared through her limb with such intensity, it brought tears to her eyes.

Then she remembered Charlie. Despite the pain, she crawled to his side to check on his condition. Still out cold. She checked for a pulse and then surveyed his injuries. He had a nasty bump on his head as well as some cuts and bruises. She opened his shirt to look for injuries and found bruising beginning to form from the beating. His breathing was shallow, but any sign of life was a relief to her.

Star could still hear laser fire coming from the forest and soldiers screaming. She suspected Pia wouldn't be long. She didn't worry about the welfare of her over an enthusiastic teammate. Although Pia was a lousy actress and at times irresponsible, she was one of the best shots in the Special Forces and one of its finest soldiers.

While she waited for Pia to return, Star tore open the pant leg of her uniform to assess the damage. Though it hurt like hell, the wound wasn't serious. She made a bandage out of the material she tore and stayed by Charlie until Pia came back.

Pia reappeared 10 minutes later, a little dirtier

than before, but seemingly unharmed. She saw her commander's leg and concern shadowed her face. "I'm sorry I took so long," she said as she kneeled over her commander's leg. "Are you okay?"

"We need to see a medic, but I think we'll live," said Star.

A look of relief washed over Pia and then a slight smile played on her lips. "When they fire, you're supposed to duck, Commander," she said with a chuckle.

As Star gave out a small laugh, she heard a ship overhead. She looked up to see the Lionex with its landing gear coming down.

The End

About the Author

Ann Marie R. Harvie has been the editor of the award winning magazine, "The Yankee Engineer," since 1992. She is also a contributing writer to the "Army Engineer Magazine" and the "Corps Environment."

She has had short stories from the "Pente Force Chronicles" series published in small press magazines over the years. Currently, stories in the series can be found on Writing.com and Scriggler. Ann Marie writes several blogs: "Stories from Out of This World," on Blogger.com and WordPress as well as "Random Thoughts of a Crazy Busy Mom" on Blogger.com.

Follow Ann Marie on Twitter @EditorYE and on LinkedIn.

www.ingramcontent.com/pod-product-compliance
Lightning Source LLC
Chambersburg PA
CBHW030640130626
46552CB00002B/938